W9-CCP-695

PATRICK CARMAN's

SKELETON CREEK

PC STUDIO

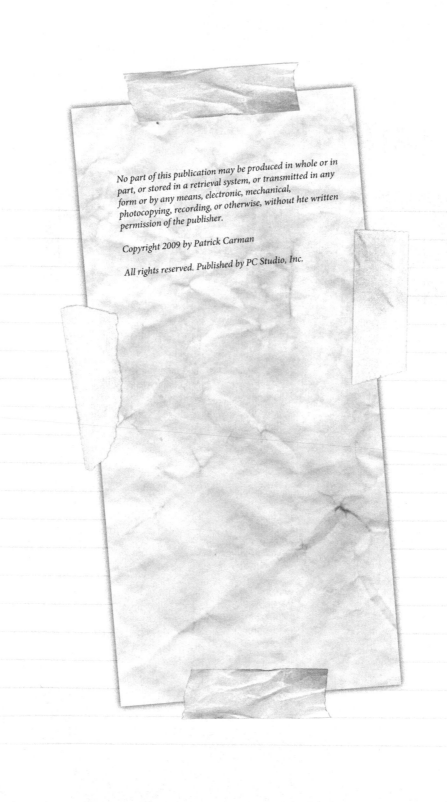

No part of this publication may be produced in whole or in part, or stored in a retrieval system, or transmitted in any form or by any means, electronic, mechanical, photocopying, recording, or otherwise, without hte written permission of the publisher.

Copyright 2009 by Patrick Carman

All rights reserved. Published by PC Studio, Inc.

Monday, September 13, 5:30 a.m.

There was a moment not long ago when I thought: <u>This is it. I'm dead.</u>

I think about that night all the time and I feel the same fear I felt then. It happened two weeks ago, but fourteen days and nights of remembering have left me more afraid and uncertain than ever.

Which I guess means it isn't over yet. Something tells me it may never truly be over.

Last night was the first time I slept in my own room since everything happened. I'd gotten in the habit of waking in the hospital to the sound of a nurse's shuffling feet, the dry chalk-dust smell of her skin, and the soft shaking of my shoulder.

<u>The doctor will visit you in a moment. He'll want you awake. Can you sit up for me, Ryan?</u>

There was no nurse or doctor or chalky smell this morning, only the early train crawling through town to wake me at half past five. But in my waking mind, it wasn't a train I heard. It was something more menacing, trying to sneak past in the early dawn, glancing down the dead-end streets, hunting.

1

I WAS SCARED — AND THEN I WAS RELIEVED — BECAUSE MY OVERACTIVE IMAGINATION HAD SETTLED BACK INTO ITS NATURAL RESTING STATE OF FEAR AND PARANOIA.

IN OTHER WORDS, I WAS BACK HOME IN SKELETON CREEK.

USUALLY WHEN THE MORNING TRAIN WAKES ME UP, I GO STRAIGHT TO MY DESK AND START WRITING BEFORE THE REST OF THE TOWN STARTS TO STIR. BUT THIS MORNING — AFTER SHAKING THE IDEA THAT SOMETHING WAS STALKING ME — I HAD A SUDDEN URGE TO LEAP FROM MY BED AND JUMP ON BOARD THE TRAIN. IT WAS A FEELING I DIDN'T EXPECT AND HADN'T THE SLIGHTEST CHANCE OF ACTING ON. BUT STILL, I WONDERED WHERE THE FEELING HAD COME FROM.

NOW, I'VE RESTED THIS JOURNAL ON A TV TRAY WITH ITS LEGS TORN OFF, PROPPED MYSELF UP IN BED ON A COUPLE OF PILLOWS, AND HAVE STARTED DOING THE ONE THING I CAN STILL DO THAT HAS ALWAYS MADE ME FEEL BETTER.

I HAVE BEGUN TO WRITE ABOUT THAT NIGHT AND ALL THAT COMES AFTER.

Monday, September 13, 6:03 a.m.

I need to take breaks. It still hurts to write. Physically, mentally, emotionally — it seems like every part of me is broken in one way or another. But I have to start doing this again. Two weeks in the hospital without a journal left me starving for words.

I have kept a lot of journals, but this one is especially important for two reasons. Reason number one: I'm not writing this for myself. I'm putting these words down for someone else to find, which is something I never do. Reason number two: I have a strong feeling this will be the last journal I ever write.

My name, in case someone finds this and cares to know who wrote it, is Ryan. I'm almost old enough to drive. (Although this would require access to a car, which I lack.) I'm told that I'm tall for my age but need to gain weight or there's no hope of making the varsity cut next year. I have a great hope that I will remain thin.

3

I CAN IMAGINE WHAT THIS MORNING WOULD HAVE BEEN LIKE BEFORE THE ACCIDENT. I WOULD BE GETTING READY FOR THE HOUR-LONG BUS RIDE TO SCHOOL. I WOULD HAVE SO MUCH TO SAY TO SARAH. AN HOUR NEXT TO HER WAS ALWAYS TIME WELL-SPENT. WE HAD SO MUCH IN COMMON, WHICH KEPT US FROM GOING COMPLETELY CRAZY IN A TOWN POPULATED BY JUST UNDER SEVEN HUNDRED PEOPLE.

I'M REALLY GOING TO MISS THOSE CONVERSATIONS WITH SARAH. I WONDER IF I'LL GET LONELY. THE TRUTH IS I DON'T EVEN KNOW IF I'M ALLOWED TO MENTION HER NAME. BUT I CAN'T STOP. I AM A WRITER. THIS IS WHAT I DO. MY TEACHERS, PARENTS, EVEN SARAH — THEY ALL SAY I WRITE TOO MUCH, THAT I'M OBSESSIVE ABOUT IT. BUT THEN, IN THE SAME BREATH, THEY CAN'T HELP BUT MENTION THAT I'M GIFTED. LIKE WHEN MRS. GARVEY TOLD ME I UNDERSTAND WORDS AND THEIR USAGE IN THE SAME WAY A PRODIGY ON THE PIANO UNDERSTANDS NOTES AND SOUNDS. BUT I HAVE A MUCH SIMPLER ANSWER, AND I'M PRETTY SURE I'M MORE RIGHT THAN MY TEACHER IS: I HAVE WRITTEN A LOT, EVERY DAY, EVERY YEAR, FOR MANY YEARS IN A ROW.

PRACTICE MAKES PERFECT.

I THINK MY FAVORITE WRITERS ARE THOSE WHO ADMITTED WHILE THEY WERE STILL ALIVE THAT THEY COULDN'T LIVE WITHOUT WRITING. JOHN STEINBECK, ERNEST HEMINGWAY, ROBERT FROST — GUYS WHO PUT WRITING UP THERE IN THE SAME CATEGORY AS AIR AND WATER. WRITE OR DIE TRYING. THAT KIND OF THINKING AGREES WITH ME.

BECAUSE HERE I AM. WRITE OR DIE TRYING.

IF I TURN BACK THE PAGES IN ALL THE JOURNALS I'VE WRITTEN, I BASICALLY FIND TWO THINGS: SCARY STORIES OF MY OWN CREATION AND THE RECORDING OF STRANGE OCCURRENCES IN SKELETON CREEK. I CAN'T SAY FOR CERTAIN WHY THIS IS SO, OTHER THAN TO FALL BACK ON THE OLD ADAGE THAT A WRITER WRITES WHAT HE KNOWS, AND I HAVE KNOWN FEAR ALL MY LIFE.

I DON'T THINK I'M A COWARD — I WOULDN'T BE IN THE POSITION I'M IN NOW IF I WAS A COWARD — BUT I AM THE SORT OF PERSON WHO OVERANALYZES, WORRIES, FRETS. WHEN I HEAR A NOISE SCRATCHING UNDER THE BED — EITHER REAL OR IMAGINED — I STARE AT THE CEILING FOR HOURS AND WONDER WHAT IT MIGHT BE THAT'S TRYING TO CLAW ITS WAY OUT. (I PICTURE IT

5

WITH FANGS, LONG BONY FINGERS, AND BULGING RED EYES.) FOR A PERSON WHO WORRIES LIKE I DO AND HAS A VIVID IMAGINATION TO MATCH, SKELETON CREEK IS THE WRONG SORT OF PLACE TO ENDURE CHILDHOOD.

I KNOW MY WRITING HAS CHANGED IN THE PAST YEAR. THE TWO KINDS OF WRITING — THE MADE-UP SCARY STORIES AND THE DOCUMENTING OF EVENTS IN SKELETON CREEK — HAVE SLOWLY BECOME ONE. I DON'T HAVE TO MAKE UP STORIES ANY LONGER, BECAUSE I'M MORE CERTAIN THAN EVER THAT THE VERY TOWN I LIVE IN IS HAUNTED.

THIS IS THE TRUTH.

AND THE TRUTH, I'VE LEARNED, CAN KILL YOU.

I'M TIRED NOW. SO TIRED.

I HAVE TO PUT THIS DOWN.

EVEN IF I CAN'T STOP THINKING ABOUT IT.

Monday, September 13, 2:00 p.m.

I have to be careful to keep this hidden.

I have to make sure nobody sees me writing in it.

They're curious enough as it is.

They're watching me enough as it is.

I'm a captive, really. I'm imprisoned in my own room.

I have no idea how much they know.

I don't even know how much I know.

I have so many questions, and no way to answer them.

There is something about having been gone for two weeks in a row that helps me see Skeleton Creek with fresh eyes. I have a new idea of what someone from the outside might think if they drove into my isolated hometown where it sits alone at the bottom of the mountains.

I like to act on these thoughts and write them down as if they are occurring. It's a curious habit I can't seem to break. Maybe things are safer when I think of them as fiction.

If I imagine myself as a person arriving in Skeleton Creek for the first time it goes something like this:

The sun has barely risen when a car door opens and a man stands at the curb looking out into the forest beyond the edge of town. There is a gray fog that hangs thick and sticky in the trees, unwilling to leave, hiding something diabolical in the woods. He gets back in his car and locks the doors, glancing down side streets through dusty windows. He wonders what has brought this little town to its knees. The place is not dead: it is not even dying for certain. Instead, the driver thinks to himself, this place has been forgotten. And he senses something else. There are secrets buried here that are best left alone.

It is then that the car turns sharply and leaves in the direction from which it came, the driver confident that the growing light of day will not shake the unforeseen dread he feels about the town at the bottom of the mountain.

THE DRIVER WOULD NOT KNOW EXACTLY WHAT IT WAS THAT SCARED HIM OFF, BUT I KNOW. SARAH KNOWS, TOO. WE KNOW THERE'S SOMETHING WRONG WITH THIS PLACE, AND MORE IMPORTANT, WE KNOW WE'RE GETTING TOO CLOSE TO WHATEVER IT IS.

SOMEONE'S COMING.

Monday, September 13, 4:30 p.m.

When did our search begin?

If I could get to my old journals, I might be able to figure out the exact date. But they're hidden, and there's no way for me to get to them in my present state. Not without help. And the only person who could help me — Sarah — isn't here anymore.

I guess our searching began with a question she asked me last summer.

"Why Skeleton Creek?"

"You mean the name?"

"Yes, the name. Why call a town Skeleton Creek? Nobody wants to visit a place with a name like that. It's bad for tourism."

"Maybe the people who named it didn't want any visitors."

"Don't you think it's weird no one wants to talk about it? It's like they're hiding something."

"You're just looking for a reason to go snooping around with your camera."

"There's something to it. A name like that has to come from somewhere."

I REMEMBER THINKING THERE WAS A STORY HIDDEN WITHIN WHAT SHE'D SAID, AND THAT I WANTED TO BE THE ONE TO WRITE THE STORY. I HAD VISIONS OF EVERYONE IN SKELETON CREEK APPLAUDING MY EFFORTS TO UNCOVER THE PAST. THE FANTASY OF CREATING SOMETHING IMPORTANT APPEALED TO ME.

WE BEGAN OUR QUEST AT THE LOCAL LIBRARY, A GLOOMY TWELVE-BY-TWELVE-FOOT ROOM AT ELM AND MAIN, OPEN ON MONDAYS AND WEDNESDAYS. IT WAS ALSO OPEN ON NEW YEAR'S DAY, CHRISTMAS DAY, AND EASTER SUNDAY, BECAUSE ACCORDING TO GLADYS MORGAN, OUR PREHISTORIC AND VERY UNHAPPY TOWN LIBRARIAN, "NOBODY COMES IN ON THOSE DAYS AND THE LIBRARY IS DEATHLY QUIET, AS A LIBRARY SHOULD BE."

GLADYS MORGAN IS NOT A FRIENDLY WOMAN. SHE STARES AT EACH PERSON SHE ENCOUNTERS IN PRECISELY THE SAME WAY: AS IF EVERYONE IN TOWN HAS JUST KICKED HER CAT ACROSS THE ROOM. SHE HAS SKIN LIKE CRUMPLED NEWSPAPER. HER LOWER LIP HAS LOST ITS SPRING AND HANGS HEAVY OVER HER CHIN. THERE IS AN ALARMING OVERBITE.

I REMEMBER THE DAY WE WALKED INTO

THE LIBRARY, THE LITTLE BELL TINKLING AT OUR ENTRY.

THE ROOM SMELLED MUSTY, AND I WASN'T CERTAIN IF IT CAME FROM THE OLD BOOKS OR FROM THE WOMAN WHO GUARDED THEM. SARAH PEPPERED GLADYS WITH QUESTIONS AS I RAN MY FINGERS ALONG THE SPINES OF THE MOST BORING BOOKS I'D EVER SEEN, UNTIL AT LAST MISS MORGAN PUT HER HAND UP AND SPOKE.

"THIS TOWN WASN'T CALLED SKELETON CREEK UNTIL 1959."

SHE REACHED BENEATH HER DESK, WHICH HAD SAT DECAYING IN THE SAME SPOT FOR A HUNDRED YEARS, AND PULLED OUT A WOODEN MILK CRATE. INSIDE WERE NEWSPAPERS, TORN AND YELLOWED.

"YOU'RE NOT THE FIRST TO ASK ABOUT THE PAST, SO I'LL ADVISE YOU LIKE I'VE DONE THE REST."

SHE GLANCED PAST THE DARK CURTAINS TO THE STREET OUTSIDE AND SHOVED THE BOX ACROSS THE DESK, LEAVING A STREAK WHERE DUST HAD BEEN LIFTED. SHE HAD A PECULIAR, SUPERSTITIOUS LOOK ON HER FACE.

"READ THEM IF YOU WANT, BUT LET IT GO AFTER THAT. BEYOND THESE YOU'LL ONLY STIR UP TROUBLE."

GLADYS took a white cloth from her pocket and removed her wire-rimmed glasses, wiping them with wrinkled hands and casting shadows across the peeling wallpaper behind her.

"I'll make a note you've checked those out. Have them back on Monday or it's a dollar a day."

THE town librarian clammed up after that, as if someone had been eavesdropping and she'd said as much as she was allowed to. But GLADYS MORGAN had given us a beginning, a thread to grab hold of. It would lead us to trouble of a kind we hadn't anticipated.

Monday, September 13, 6:40 p.m.

I stopped there for a while because all of this has made me think of Sarah.

I wonder if she were here whether she'd be telling what happened the same way. Not writing it down — "Not my thing," she always said. But I wonder if she would remember things differently.

I look back, I see warning signs.

Sarah looks back, she sees invitations.

I miss her.

I blame her.

I'm scared for her.

I'm scared <u>of</u> her. Not a lot. But some.

It was wrong of me to write "I blame her."

It's not like she tricked me into anything.

I went along willingly.

I was the one who put my life on the line. Even if I didn't realize I was doing it.

I guess what I'm saying is that none of this would have happened if Sarah hadn't been around.

Now —

I do miss her.

And I do blame her.

14

And I'm sure her story would be different from mine.

But where was I? Oh, yeah — we began reading through the stack of newspapers. From 1947 to 1958, there had been a monthly paper for the 1200 residents. The paper had an uninspiring name — The Linkford Bi-Weekly — but it told us what our town had once been called. Linkford. It had a nice ring to it, or so I thought at the time.

The title of the paper became more interesting in 1959 when it was renamed The Skeleton Creek Irregular. (This was an appropriate name, for we could only find a handful of papers dated between 1959 and 1975, when the publisher fled to Reno, Nevada, and took the printing press with him.)

Linkford sat alone on a long, empty road at the bottom of a forested mountain in the western state of Oregon. It surprised us to discover that an official from the New York Gold and Silver Company had suggested the town name be changed to Skeleton Creek. Actually, we were fairly dumbstruck that anyone from New York would take an interest in our town at all.

"Why in the world would a big city mining company want to change the name of the town?" I remember asking Sarah.

"It's that monstrous machine in the woods," she answered. "The dredge. I bet that has something to do with it. They probably owned it."

The dredge. Already, we were headed toward the dredge. I'll bet Sarah was planning things in her mind even way back then.

Not knowing the consequences.

Just thinking about the mystery.

We pieced together the small bits of information we could gather from those who would talk (hardly anyone) and the newspapers we'd been given (less than thirty in all, none complete editions). We had gone as far as creepy old Gladys Morgan said we should go, and yet we kept pulling on the thread we'd taken hold of.

Of course, I was less enthusiastic than Sarah at first, knowing that if our parents discovered what we were doing, they would demand that we stop prying into other people's business. Privacy has long been the religion of our town.

But Sarah can be persuasive, especially when she finds something she wants to record on film. She could be consumed by filmmaking in the same way that I am with writing. Our creative obsessions seem to draw us together like magnets, and I had a hard time pulling away when she was determined to drag me along.

And so we kept digging.

Of course, I know where all of this is going. I just have to get it down on paper. One last time.

MONDAY, SEPTEMBER 13, 8:30 P.M.

REMEMBER.

I HAVE TO TRY TO REMEMBER ALL THE DETAILS.

THEY COULD STILL BE IMPORTANT.

IT FEELS LIKE MIDNIGHT: IT'S ONLY 8:30.

HOW DID THIS HAPPEN TO ME?

STOP, RYAN. GO BACK.

REMEMBER.

EVEN IF YOU KNOW HOW IT'S GOING TO FEEL.

EVEN IF YOU DON'T HAVE ANY OF THE ANSWERS.

THERE WERE SMALL ANNOUNCEMENTS IN FOUR OF THE NEWSPAPERS THAT ALLUDED TO SOMETHING CALLED THE CROSSBONES. THEY WERE CRYPTIC ADS IN NATURE, CONTAINING A SERIES OF SYMBOLS AND BRIEF TEXT THAT SEEMED TO HAVE NO MEANING. ONE SUCH MESSAGE READ AS FOLLOWS: THE FLOOR AND 7TH, FOUR PAST THE NINE ON DOOR NUMBER TWO. CROSSBONES. WHO IN THEIR RIGHT MIND COULD DECIPHER SUCH NONSENSE? CERTAINLY NOT US.

ALL OF THE ADVERTISEMENTS CAME BETWEEN THE YEARS OF 1959 AND 1963 AND ALL APPEARED IN THE SKELETON CREEK IRREGULAR. THEN, IN 1964, THEY

CEASED ALTOGETHER, AS IF THEY HAD NEVER EXISTED AT ALL. BUT THE SAME SYMBOLS COULD STILL BE FOUND IN VARIOUS PLACES. ONE OF THE SYMBOLS — TWO BONES TANGLED IN BARBED WIRE — COULD BE SEEN ABOVE THE DOOR TO THE LOCAL BAR, ON A SIGNPOST AT THE EDGE OF TOWN, AND AGAIN CARVED INTO A VERY OLD TREE ALONG A PATHWAY INTO THE WOODS. IT MADE US WONDER IF THE MEMBERS OF THE CROSSBONES WERE STILL MEETING. WHO HAD BEEN PART OF THE SOCIETY? WHAT WAS ITS FUNCTION? WERE THERE STILL ACTIVE MEMBERS — AND, IF SO, WHO WERE THEY?

OUR TRAIL DEAD-ENDED WITH THE ADVERTISEMENTS.

WE SEARCHED RELENTLESSLY ONLINE FOR CLUES TO OUR TOWN'S PAST. NEW YORK GOLD AND SILVER WAS BANKRUPTED OVER ENVIRONMENTAL LAWSUITS, AND IT SEEMED TO VANISH INTO THIN AIR AFTER 1985. BUT THIS DIDN'T KEEP US FROM SNEAKING DOWN THE DARK PATH INTO THE WOODS TO EXAMINE WHAT WAS LEFT BEHIND.

DO I WISH WE'D NEVER GONE DOWN THAT PATH?

YES.

NO.

I DON'T KNOW.

IT'S TOO COMPLICATED.

OR IS IT? NONE OF THIS WOULD HAVE HAPPENED IF WE'D STAYED AWAY FROM THE DREDGE.

THE DREDGE IS A CRUCIAL PART OF THE TOWN'S DREARY PAST. IT SITS ALONE AND UNVISITED IN THE DEEPEST PART OF THE DARK WOODS. THE DREDGE, WE DISCOVERED, WAS A TERRIBLE MACHINE. ITS PURPOSE WAS TO FIND GOLD, AND ITS METHOD WAS GROTESQUE. 24 HOURS A DAY, 365 DAYS A YEAR, THE DREDGE SAT IN A MUDDY LAKE OF ITS OWN MAKING. IT DUG DEEP INTO THE EARTH AND HAULED GARGANTUAN BUCKETS OF STONE AND DEBRIS INTO ITSELF. NOTHING ESCAPED ITS RELENTLESS APPETITE. EVERYTHING WENT INSIDE THE DREDGE. TREES AND BOULDERS AND DIRT CLODS THE SIZE OF MY HEAD WERE SIFTED AND SHAKEN WITH A NEAR—DEAFENING RACKET, AND THEN IT WAS ALL SPIT OUT BEHIND IN PILES OF RUBBLE TEN FEET HIGH. A TAIL OF RUIN — MILES AND MILES IN LENGTH — ALL SO TINY BITS OF GOLD COULD BE SIFTED OUT.

THE TRENCH THAT WAS LEFT BEHIND AS THE DREDGE MARCHED FORWARD FORMED THE TWENTY—TWO—MILE

STREAMBED THAT ZIGZAGS WILDLY ALONG THE EDGE OF TOWN AND UP INTO THE LOW PART OF THE MOUNTAIN. THE GUTTED EARTH FILLED WITH WATER, AND THE BANKS WERE STREWN WITH WHITEWASHED LIMBS THAT LOOKED LIKE BROKEN BONES.

THE NEW WATERWAY TORN FROM EARTH AND STONE WAS CALLED SKELETON CREEK BY A MAN IN A SUIT FROM NEW YORK. MAYBE IT HAD BEEN A JOKE, MAYBE NOT. EITHER WAY THE NAME STUCK. SOON AFTER, THE TOWN TOOK THE NAME AS WELL. IT WOULD SEEM THAT NEW YORK GOLD AND SILVER HELD ENOUGH SWAY OVER LINKFORD TO CHANGE THE TOWN NAME TO WHATEVER IT WANTED.

THE GREATEST DISCOVERY — OR THE WORST, DEPENDING ON HOW YOU LOOK AT IT — THAT SARAH AND I MADE INVOLVED THE UNTIMELY DEATH OF A WORKMAN ON THE DREDGE. THERE WAS ONLY ONE MENTION OF THE INCIDENT IN THE NEWSPAPER, AND NOTHING ANYWHERE ELSE. OLD JOE BUSH IS WHAT THEY CALLED HIM, SO I CAN ONLY CONCLUDE THAT HE WAS NOT A YOUNG MAN. OLD JOE BUSH HAD LET HIS PANT LEG GET CAUGHT IN THE GEARS, AND THE

MACHINERY OF THE DREDGE HAD PULLED HIM THROUGH, CRUSHING HIS LEG BONE INTO GRAVEL. THEN THE DREDGE SPIT HIM OUT INTO THE GRIMY WATER. HIS LEG WAS DEMOLISHED, AND UNDER THE DEAFENING SOUND IN THE DARK NIGHT, NO ONE HEARD HIM SCREAM.

OLD JOE BUSH NEVER EMERGED FROM THE BLACK POND BELOW.

MONDAY, SEPTEMBER 13, 10:00 P.M.

OKAY. I THINK EVERYONE IS ASLEEP NOW.

IT'S AS SAFE AS IT'S GOING TO GET.

LATE LAST NIGHT, ON MY ARRIVAL HOME FROM THE HOSPITAL, I WAS REUNITED WITH MY COMPUTER. THIS MAY SEEM LIKE A STRANGE THING TO WRITE, BUT THE ALREADY WALLOPING POWER OF A COMPUTER IS MAGNIFIED EVEN MORE FOR PEOPLE LIKE ME IN A SMALL, ISOLATED TOWN. IT IS THE LINK TO SOMETHING NOT BORING, NOT DULL, NOT DREARY. IT HAS ALWAYS BEEN ESPECIALLY TRUE IN MY CASE BECAUSE SARAH IS CONSTANTLY MAKING VIDEOS, POSTING THEM, AND ASKING ME TO TAKE NOTICE.

ONE SIMPLE CLICK — THAT'S ALL IT CAN TAKE FOR YOUR LIFE TO CHANGE.

SOMETIMES FOR THE BETTER.

SOMETIMES FOR THE MUCH WORSE.

BUT WE DON'T THINK ABOUT THAT.

NO, WE JUST CLICK.

THERE IS A CERTAIN VIDEO SHE MADE FIFTEEN DAYS AGO, A DAY BEFORE THE ACCIDENT. THIS VIDEO IS LIKE A ROAD SIGN THAT SAYS YOU'VE GONE TOO

23

FAR. TURN BACK. I AM AFRAID TO LOOK AT IT AGAIN, BECAUSE I KNOW THAT AFTER I WATCH IT, I'M GOING TO HAVE EVEN MORE OF A BEWILDERING SENSE THAT MY LIFE HAS BEEN BROKEN INTO TWO PARTS — EVERYTHING THAT CAME BEFORE THIS VIDEO, AND EVERYTHING THAT WOULD COME AFTER.

As MUCH AS I DON'T WANT TO, I'M GOING TO STOP WRITING NOW. THERE IS A SAFETY IN WRITING LATE INTO THE NIGHT, BUT I CAN'T PUT OFF WATCHING IT AGAIN. I HAVE TO SEE IT ONCE MORE, NOW THAT THINGS HAVE CHANGED FOR THE WORSE.

IT MIGHT HELP ME.

IT MIGHT NOT.

BUT I HAVE TO DO IT.

I HAVE TO.

I'M AFRAID.

IT'S SO SIMPLE. JUST GO TO SARAH'S NAME ONLINE. SARAHFINCHER.COM. ENTER THE PASSWORD HOUSEOFUSHER. THEN CLICK RETURN.

ONE CLICK.

DO IT, RYAN.

DO IT.

24

SARAHFINCHER.COM
PASSWORD:
HOUSEOFUSHER

MONDAY, SEPTEMBER 13, 11:00 P.M.

SARAH WENT TO THE DREDGE WITHOUT ME THAT NIGHT.
WHAT WAS MY EXCUSE? <u>HOMEWORK.</u> SHE KNEW IT
WAS A LIE, AND I KNEW IT WAS A LIE, AND INSTEAD OF
BEING MAD, SARAH WENT AHEAD WITHOUT ME LIKE SHE
ALWAYS DID WHEN I BALKED AT AN OPPORTUNITY FOR
ADVENTURE. DID I GET ANY HOMEWORK DONE? NO. I
JUST WAITED FOR HER TO GET BACK, FOR HER TO SEND
WORD SHE WAS OKAY.

THEN THE PASSWORD APPEARED IN MY INBOX. I
WAS GLAD TO KNOW SARAH WAS SAFE, BUT I DIDN'T
KNOW WHAT TO MAKE OF THE CREEPY VIDEO SHE'D
SENT ME.

I WATCHED IT ABOUT TEN TIMES THAT NIGHT. I SAT AT
MY DESK WONDERING IF IT WAS SOMETHING SHE'D
CONCOCTED TO SCARE THE WITS OUT OF ME. THAT
WOULD HAVE BEEN EXPECTED, SINCE I'D REFUSED TO GO
WITH HER INTO THE WOODS. SHE WAS ALWAYS DOING
THAT — HOAXING ME INTO FEELING GUILTY.

THE NEXT MORNING, I WALKED DOWN TO HER HOUSE
WITH THE INTENT OF CONGRATULATING HER ON GIVING
ME A GOOD SCARE. I WANTED TO KNOW HOW SHE'D

GOTTEN THE EFFECT OF THE SCARY FACE IN THE
WINDOW. BUT THE CONVERSATION DIDN'T GO AS I'D
EXPECTED.

"YOU THINK I MADE IT UP?"

SHE SAID IT LIKE SHE COULDN'T BELIEVE I'D EVEN
THINK SUCH A THING. LIKE SHE HADN'T DONE IT TO ME A
MILLION TIMES BEFORE.

I THOUGHT IT WAS STILL PART OF THE ACT.

"DON'T GET ME WRONG," I SAID. "IT'S SOME OF
YOUR BEST WORK. YOU REALLY SCARED ME WITH
THOSE GEAR SOUNDS AND — WHAT WAS THAT — A MAN
AT THE WINDOW? YOU MUST HAVE HAD HELP FROM
SOMEONE. WHO HELPED YOU?"

SHE SHOOK HER HEAD. I CAN REMEMBER IT SO
CLEARLY.

"ALL I DID WAS WALK INTO THE WOODS WITH MY
CAMERA. NO ONE HELPED ME DO ANYTHING."

"YOU'RE SERIOUS?"

THERE HAD BEEN A LONG PAUSE, FOLLOWED BY A
FAMILIAR LOOK OF DETERMINATION.

"IF YOU DON'T BELIEVE ME, LET'S GO BACK TONIGHT
AND YOU CAN SEE FOR YOURSELF."

If this were a video, not a journal, I'd have to stop. I'd have to rewind. I'd have to play that line again.

"If you don't believe me, let's go back tonight and you can see for yourself."

And again.

"If you don't believe me, let's go back tonight and you can see for yourself."

I didn't know what it would lead to. How could I have?

She didn't even ask. It wasn't, "Do you want to go back tonight and see for yourself?"

No, she was smarter than that.

She didn't give me a chance to say no.

"If you don't believe me, let's go back tonight and you can see for yourself."

We watched the video twice more on her laptop, and both times a chill ran up my spine. It seemed real, and usually when I called Sarah's bluff, she admitted it. Besides, I asked myself, how could she have created something so elaborate and so real? Even for someone of Sarah's editing skill, it seemed impossible.

I believed her.

"Tonight at midnight," she said. "Meet me at the trailhead and we'll go together."

"You're sure about this?"

"Are you kidding? This town is mind-numbingly dull. We're going to die of boredom if we're not careful. Finally, something interesting is happening. Imagine what a great story this will make! All this stuff we're digging up, and now this weird — I don't know what to call it — this phantom at the dredge. It's not a question of whether we want to go back or not. We <u>have to</u> go back."

This was Sarah at her most persuasive. She said it with such urgency — no doubt because it involved her filming, the main thing that took the edge off her boredom.

I have a theory about this. I think what I do is safer than what Sarah does. I can write about whatever I want — monsters, ghosts, arms falling off, people buried alive — and it doesn't matter what I write because it all comes from the safety of my own imagination. But filming requires that there be something to film, and that has a way of leading into real danger.

Tuesday, September 14, 1:25 a.m.

. . . but I can't sleep.

It's not the disturbing sound of rusted gears set in motion (though I keep hearing them) or the moving shadows in the upper room of the dredge (I have decided that I <u>hate</u> shadows). What scares me the most is listening to Sarah. I can hear the fear in Sarah's voice. Up until I saw that video I'd never heard her sound like that before.

She just doesn't get scared. When she purchased her first video camera, Sarah interviewed a drifter walking through town. This was a terrible idea. The man was not well-dressed, to say the very least. All of his possessions were tied to his back in black plastic garbage bags and he carried a sign that read <u>Los Angeles</u>, if you please.

Sarah talks to strangers all the time without thinking twice about it. She peers into parked cars, eavesdrops in the café, and occasionally tries to sneak into the bar (for lively conversation, not drinks).

When we were eleven, Sarah convinced me we could climb up a steep ravine to the very top. She was right — we made it — but we couldn't get back down without the help of a park ranger, her father, my father, and half the volunteer fire department (three lumberjacks and a retired police officer). This event preceded my earliest memory of stern fatherly advice: <u>Find some other friends. Try out for football if you want, but stop spending so much time with Sarah. She'll only get you into trouble.</u>

There was the hitchhiking incident, in which Sarah convinced me we needed to visit the metropolis a hundred miles away so that we could "observe city dwellers in their native environment." When night approached and we couldn't find a ride back home, we were forced to call my dad. A second warning was offered on the long ride home. <u>You two had better stop acting like idiots. It's only a matter of time before one of you gets hurt.</u>

There was very little else said.

And then, only a month ago, we were caught trying to break into the library on a Thursday night. It was supposed to be closed and we had hoped to find more old newspapers, but we found Gladys Morgan instead. She was sitting in the dark with a shotgun pointed at the door, reading The Sound and the Fury (one of the dullest books ever written). We were very lucky she recognized us. Otherwise she would have filled us so full of buckshot we'd never set foot in a restaurant again without someone mistaking us for Swiss cheese (her words, not mine). She also told us we were dumber than two bags full of rocks. Then she called our parents.

As you can probably imagine, our two sets of parents have long preferred the idea of us staying as far away from each other as possible. It is this long history of trouble that made them respond so forcefully when something really bad finally did happen.

It's why, if they have their way, Sarah and I will never see each other again.

TUESDAY, SEPTEMBER 14, 2:00 A.M.

I HAVE JUST MADE THE MISTAKE OF CHECKING MY EMAIL. THIS IS A BAD IDEA IN THE MIDDLE OF THE NIGHT. I SHOULD KNOW BETTER. BUT THERE WAS NOTHING WHEN I CHECKED FOR MESSAGES EARLIER, NOT EVEN A MEASLY WELCOME HOME. ALL DAY I'VE BEEN WONDERING IF MY PARENTS FOUND SOMETHING AND DELETED IT. IT'S HARD TO TELL HOW CLOSELY THEY'RE MONITORING EVERYTHING.

BUT NOW SOMETHING'S SLIPPED THROUGH. AND I'LL ADMIT — I DEBATED WHETHER OR NOT TO OPEN IT. BECAUSE I KNEW — THE MOMENT SARAH AND I WERE IN CONTACT, IT WOULD START ALL OVER AGAIN.

STILL, HOW COULD I RESIST? I'D NEVER BEEN ABLE TO BEFORE.

"LEARN FROM YOUR MISTAKES," PART OF ME WAS SAYING.

"THEY WEREN'T MISTAKES," ANOTHER PART OF ME WAS SAYING.

AND, OF COURSE, CURIOSITY WON. OR MAYBE IT WAS FRIENDSHIP THAT WON.

I OPENED HER EMAIL.

Ryan,

I'm so sorry about what happened. At least you're home again — that makes me feel a little better. I've hardly left my room. I know they've said we can't see each other because of what happened. I know I'm not supposed to contact you. But it's important that you see this. Please, just drop whatever it is you're doing and watch.

Sarah.

I LOVED THAT — JUST DROP WHATEVER IT IS YOU'RE DOING. SUCH A SARAH THING TO SAY. LIKE I HADN'T SPENT THE PAST TWO WEEKS GLUED TO A HOSPITAL MATTRESS, WONDERING WHEN THE PAIN WAS GOING TO GO AWAY.

THERE WAS A PASSWORD ATTACHED TO THE BOTTOM OF THE EMAIL. THERAVEN.

I HAVE TO SAY, I DON'T APPRECIATE HER PASSWORDS. IT'S LIKE SHE'S TRYING TO MAKE THINGS EVEN SCARIER THAN THEY ALREADY ARE. THINGS ARE CREEPY ENOUGH WITHOUT BRINGING EDGAR ALLAN POE BACK FROM THE DEAD. SHE KNEW I'D FIND HER

MESSAGE IN THE MIDDLE OF THE NIGHT WHILE MY PARENTS WERE ASLEEP AND EVERY SHADOW LOOKED LIKE SOMETHING OUT TO GET ME.

Once upon a midnight dreary, while I pondered weak and weary,
Over many a quaint and curious volume of forgotten lore,
While I nodded, nearly napping, suddenly there came a tapping,
As of some one gently rapping, rapping at my chamber door.

Does she even know about this poem or is she just pulling these passwords out of thin air?

Something happened fifteen nights ago that has changed everything. I'm sure what Sarah wants me to watch has something to do with that night. It's why I'm writing this down, because my lingering fear has turned to constant alarm these past weeks. I have a dreadful feeling someone is watching me all the time, that someone or something will open the creaking

DOOR TO MY ROOM IN THE COLD NIGHT AND DO AWAY WITH ME. I WANT THERE TO BE SOME KIND OF RECORD.

If I WONDERED WHETHER OR NOT I SHOULD OPEN THE EMAIL, NOW THERE'S NO QUESTION IN MY MIND.

ONCE YOU'RE IN, YOU'RE IN.

ONCE YOU'RE CAUGHT, YOU'RE CAUGHT.

I HAVE TO WATCH WHAT SHE SENT. I HAVE TO WATCH IT RIGHT NOW.

SARAHFINCHER.COM
PASSWORD:
THERAVEN

TUESDAY, SEPTEMBER 14, 9:00 A.M.

LAST NIGHT I SORT OF FREAKED OUT. AFTER I WATCHED THE VIDEO I THINK I HAD THE SECOND MOMENT OF REAL TERROR IN MY LIFE.

THE FIRST WAS HAVING IT HAPPEN TO ME.

THE SECOND WAS SEEING IT.

WHAT WAS SARAH THINKING, SENDING THIS TO ME? I'VE BEEN SCARED BEFORE — ACTUALLY, LET'S BE HONEST, I'M SCARED MOST OF THE TIME. THERE'S A BLIND MAN WHO SITS OUTSIDE THE RAINBOW BAR AND WHEN I WALK BY HE FOLLOWS MY EVERY MOVE WITH A CLOUDED WHITE EYE — THAT SCARES ME. AT HOME I HEAR CREAKING STAIRS AT NIGHT WHEN IT SHOULD BE QUIET, AND I CALL OUT BUT NO ONE ANSWERS. THAT SCARES ME. THE THING LIVING UNDER MY BED, GLADYS AND HER SHOTGUN, THE WOODS AT NIGHT. IT ALL SCARES ME, AND IT'S ALL LIKE CLOTHES IN A DRYER THAT JUST KEEP ROLLING AROUND IN MY HEAD FROM ONE DAY TO THE NEXT.

BUT WATCHING THAT VIDEO LAST NIGHT WAS DIFFERENT. I COULDN'T EVEN WRITE. I TURNED ON AS MANY LIGHTS AS I COULD REACH. I TURNED ON THE RADIO AND LISTENED TO THE CHURCH CHANNEL UNTIL A

MAN STARTED TALKING ABOUT SPIRITUAL WARFARE,
WHICH SHARPENED MY FEAR EVEN MORE.

THE REASON THE VIDEO TERRIFIED ME WAS BECAUSE
IT MADE ME REMEMBER THAT NIGHT. SINCE IT
HAPPENED, I'VE HAD ONLY A FRAGMENTED MEMORY,
LITTLE BITS AND PIECES. BUT NOW I REMEMBER
SOMETHING MORE ABOUT THAT NIGHT. I REMEMBER WHAT
I SAW THAT MADE ME FALL. IT WAS THERE IN THE
CAMERA LENS AT THE END.

IT WAS WATCHING ME.

IT'S ALWAYS WATCHING ME.

TUESDAY, SEPTEMBER 14, 10:15 A.M.

I REMEMBER WAKING UP IN THE HOSPITAL. WHAT IT WAS LIKE.

ONE MOMENT I WAS FALLING. THEN I SAW SARAH'S FACE HOVERING IN THE DIM LIGHT BUT COULDN'T HEAR WHAT SHE WAS TRYING TO SAY. IT FELT LIKE THE BONES IN MY LEG HAD EXPLODED.

THEN I WAS OUT. WHEN I OPENED MY EYES I ACTUALLY EXPECTED TO SEE THE CEILING OF MY ROOM AND SMELL MY DAD'S COFFEE BREWING DOWNSTAIRS. MY HEAD LOLLED TO ONE SIDE AND THERE SAT MY PARENTS, GLASSY-EYED FROM SLEEPLESSNESS.

I REMEMBER ASKING, "WHAT'S GOING ON?" AND MY MOM JUMPING UP AND SAYING, "RYAN! GO GET THE NURSE, PAUL — GO ON!"

MY DAD SMILED AT ME, OPENED THE DOOR, AND RAN FROM THE ROOM. I HEARD THE MUFFLED SOUND OF HIM YELLING FOR A NURSE OUTSIDE THE DOOR. MOM LEANED OVER THE BED RAIL AND HELD MY HAND.

"WHERE ARE WE?" I ASKED.

"YOU HAD AN ACCIDENT, BUT YOU'RE AWAKE NOW — YOU'RE AWAKE AND YOU'RE GOING TO BE JUST FINE."

40

"How long have I been asleep?"

"The nurse — she'll bring the doctor, he'll want to talk to you. Just stay awake. No more sleeping until your dad comes back with the nurse. Okay?"

She squeezed my hand pretty hard, as if it might help keep me from drifting off.

At that point, I didn't have any memory of what had happened to me. There were little bits and pieces, but nothing concrete.

When the doctor came in, I asked if I could use the bathroom and he told me that if I wanted to I could just go ahead and pee. Certain embarrassing arrangements had been made when I was admitted.

"How long have I been asleep?"

"According to your chart you were nonresponsive when they found you at 12:45 a.m. So you've been asleep — or, more accurately, you've been in an unconscious state — for about fifty-five hours."

"So you're saying I've been in a coma?"

"IF YOU WANT TO BE DRAMATIC, THEN, YES, YOU'VE BEEN IN A COMA. YOU TOOK A PRETTY GOOD FALL. IT'S AMAZING YOU'RE ALIVE AND WELL ENOUGH TO TELL ABOUT IT."

"WHY CAN'T I MOVE MY LEG?"

"BECAUSE WE'VE SURROUNDED IT WITH A BIG BERTHA — A REALLY BIG PLASTER CAST. I'M AFRAID IT WILL BE AWHILE BEFORE YOU CAN WALK ON IT AGAIN."

I BEGAN TO FALL ASLEEP IN THE HOSPITAL BED. MY MOM SHOOK MY SHOULDERS AND YELLED AT ME AND THE SMELL OF OLD BICYCLE TIRES WENT AWAY. I TRIED HARDER TO STAY AWAKE AFTER THAT BECAUSE MY HEAD HURT AND HAVING MY MOM SHOUT IN MY FACE MADE IT HURT EVEN MORE.

EVENTUALLY THEY TOOK MOST OF THE TUBES OUT OF MY BODY (INCLUDING THE ONE THAT LET ME STAY IN BED TO USE THE BATHROOM). I TOOK SOME RIDES IN A WHEELCHAIR, AND MY PARENTS STARTED TO TALK TO ME. TALKING WITH THEM WAS NICE AT FIRST, BECAUSE THEY WERE TRULY HAPPY I WAS OKAY. BUT THEN I ASKED ABOUT SARAH AND THEY BOTH TOOK DEEP BREATHS AND GOT SERIOUS ON ME.

"WE DON'T WANT YOU SEEING HER ANYMORE,"
DAD SAID.

"BUT SHE'S MY BEST FRIEND," I PROTESTED.

MOM TOOK ONE LOOK AT ME AND I COULD TELL
WHAT SHE WAS THINKING: <u>WHAT KIND OF BEST FRIEND
NEARLY KILLS YOU</u>?

"THEN YOU'LL HAVE TO FIND A NEW FRIEND," DAD
SAID. "WE'RE SERIOUS THIS TIME, RYAN. IF YOU CAN'T
STAY AWAY FROM EACH OTHER, WE'LL MOVE. I'LL
TRANSFER TO THE CITY AND WE'LL SELL THE HOUSE.
WE DON'T WANT TO, BUT WE WILL."

"WHAT ARE YOU SAYING?"

"WE'RE SAYING YOU CAN'T SEE SARAH ANYMORE,"
SAID MY MOTHER. "YOU'RE NOT TO CONTACT HER —
NO EMAIL, NO PHONE CALLS — AND SHE WON'T BE
COMING AROUND WHEN WE GO HOME. HER PARENTS
AGREE WITH US. IT'S THE BEST THING FOR A WHILE."

"THE BEST THING FOR WHO?"

"YOU WERE OUT IN THE WOODS IN THE MIDDLE OF
THE NIGHT, BREAKING INTO PRIVATE PROPERTY," SAID MY
DAD. HE WAS TALKING MORE THAN USUAL AND FOR
ONCE I WISHED HE'D SHUT UP. "YOU NEARLY FELL TO

YOUR DEATH! I THINK IT'S FAIR TO SAY THAT KEEPING HER AWAY FROM YOU IS BEST FOR EVERYONE, INCLUDING YOU."

"IT WASN'T HER FAULT THIS TIME. IT WAS ME — IT WAS MY IDEA."

"ALL THE MORE REASON TO KEEP YOU TWO APART." MY DAD WAS ON A ROLL. "BOTH YOUR BRAINS GO BATTY WHEN YOU'RE TOGETHER. THERE'S TALK IN SKELETON CREEK OF BURNING THAT DREDGE TO THE GROUND. THE POLICE SPENT A WHOLE DAY DOWN THERE LOCKING IT UP TIGHT SO NO ONE ELSE TRIES TO GET IN. THAT THING IS A DEATH TRAP."

AFTER THAT, MY PARENTS WENT QUIET. NEITHER OF THEM ARE TALKATIVE FOLKS — NO ONE WHO LIVES IN SKELETON CREEK TALKS VERY MUCH. THEY'D LAID DOWN THE LAW ABOUT SARAH, AND THAT WAS THAT. I HAD TO STAY THERE IN THE HOSPITAL FOR ANOTHER TEN DAYS. I COULDN'T GET ONLINE AND MY PARENTS WOULDN'T LET ME USE THE PHONE.

WHAT WOULD THEY DO IF THEY KNEW SARAH WAS CONTACTING ME? THEY'D SELL THE HOUSE, THAT'S WHAT THEY'D DO.

Tuesday, September 14, 11:00 a.m.

Mom just checked up on me. The computer was safely off.

She has no idea.

Or maybe she does.

I wonder if my mom is sneakier than she looks.

The day after I woke up in the hospital, the police came to my room and asked me a lot of questions. They wanted to know if I was trying to steal anything, who else was involved, why I'd done it, did I remember any details about what happened. I didn't tell them anything they didn't already know or couldn't figure out on their own. I went to the dredge, I fell, I got a serious concussion and shattered my leg. What else was I going to say? That I was looking for a phantom and might have found one? I had a strong feeling if I said anything like that they'd move me out of the hospital and into the psych ward.

As it turns out, my mental health was the very reason why they kept me for so many days. I could have gone home a week earlier, but

THERE WAS A PSYCHIATRIST WHO KEPT STOPPING BY. MY DAD WAS BACK AT WORK BUT MY MOM WAS STILL HANGING AROUND. SHE LEFT THE ROOM WHENEVER THE PSYCHIATRIST CAME IN. SHE (THE PSYCHIATRIST) WAS PRETTY, IN A BUTTON-DOWN SORT OF WAY. SHE HAD RED HAIR AND GLASSES AND A NOTEPAD. SHE ASKED ME IF I'D BEEN TAKING ANY DRUGS OR DRINKING. SHE ASKED WHAT I DID WITH MY FREE TIME AND ABOUT SARAH. SHE WONDERED IF SHE COULD READ SOME OF MY STORIES, AND I POLITELY DECLINED. I DIDN'T WANT HER DIGGING AROUND IN MY STUFF. I WAS PRETTY SURE IT WOULDN'T LOOK GOOD IF SHE FOUND MY PARANOID RANTINGS ABOUT SKELETON CREEK.

WHEN THEY FINALLY LET ME GO HOME, I HAD THE DISTINCT FEELING I'D BARELY PASSED SOME SORT OF EMOTIONAL EXAM THEY'D RUN ME THROUGH. IT FELT A LITTLE LIKE STANDARDIZED TESTING AT SCHOOL, LIKE I'D SORT OF PASSED BUT NOT REALLY, AND ANYWAY, I'D NEVER KNOW FOR SURE HOW I DID BECAUSE THEY WOULDN'T TELL ME. IT WAS AN EMPTY FEELING.

OKAY, I KNOW I'M AVOIDING SOMETHING. I'M WRITING QUICKLY, BUT I'M ALSO DODGING WHAT I REALLY SHOULD

46

BE WRITING ABOUT. NOW I'M BACK TO THE PRESENT —
CAN I AVOID IT ANY LONGER? IF I GET IT DOWN ON
PAPER, IT WILL MAKE IT REAL. BUT MAYBE IF I WRITE IT
DOWN, I'LL FEAR IT LESS. THIS STRATEGY OFTEN
WORKS FOR ME WHEN I'M SCARED. WRITING THE THINGS
I'M SCARED OF — ESPECIALLY IF I TURN THEM INTO A
STORY — MAKES THEM FEEL AS IF THEY'VE BEEN
RELEGATED TO THE PAGE AND I CAN ALLOW MYSELF TO
WORRY LESS ABOUT THEM IN REAL LIFE.

    SO HERE GOES.

    THERE WAS A PRESENCE UPSTAIRS WITH ME IN THE
DREDGE BEFORE IT WALKED IN FRONT OF SARAH'S
CAMERA LENS. I WAS EXAMINING THE RUSTED GEARS,
TRYING TO IMAGINE HOW THEY COULD POSSIBLY SPRING
TO LIFE. THE RUST CAME OFF ON MY FINGERS. (DAYS
LATER, MOM WOULD ASK ME ABOUT THE ORANGE MARK
ON MY PANTS WHERE I'D WIPED THE RUST OFF, AND I
WOULDN'T HAVE AN ANSWER FOR HER. I GUESS I HAVE
ONE NOW.)

    JUST AS I WIPED MY FINGERS, I TURNED TOWARD
THE DARKENED PATH OF BOARDS THAT LED AWAY
FROM THE GEARS WHERE OLD JOE BUSH HAD WORKED.

There was a long, wide belt that ran into the black.

And sitting on the belt was a hand.

It was attached to an arm,

The arm to a body,

And the body was moving toward me.

There was a faint light all around the body as it moved closer to me.

I can see it now.

I am seeing it.

It was a silhouette. All in black, so I couldn't make out a face. But the body was large. Whoever — whatever — this was, it was big and slow. It stepped forward, steadying itself on the wide belt as it came, and it dragged its other leg behind.

I remember now how I realized three things all at once. The first was that I couldn't speak. I don't know if it was some force of darkness that constricted my throat or if it was simply pure terror, but either way, the best I could do was keep breathing. (Even that, I now recall, came with great effort.) The second thing — and this

48

ONE WAS WORSE THAN THE FIRST — WAS THAT I FOUND MYSELF TRAPPED. I WAS BACKED UP AGAINST THE WOODEN RAIL BEHIND THE GEARS, WHICH WAS A CORNER SECTION OF THE DREDGE THAT LOOKED OUT OVER THE BOTTOM LEVEL. THIS THING THAT WAS AFTER ME HAD ME CORNERED. THE LAST REALIZATION I HAD — WORSE THAN THE FIRST TWO PUT TOGETHER — WAS THAT ALL MY TERRIBLE NIGHTMARES HAD FINALLY COME TRUE. IN THE BACK OF MY MIND, THERE HAD ALWAYS BEEN THIS ONE IMPORTANT FACT: NONE OF THE MONSTERS I'D IMAGINED OVER THE YEARS HAD EVER REALLY COME TO GET ME. BUT NOW I SAW THAT IT WAS TRUE — THERE REALLY WAS A MONSTER, AND IT REALLY WAS GOING TO SCARE ME TO DEATH.

WHEN IT WAS CLOSE ENOUGH TO TOUCH ME, I SAW THE SHADOW OF ITS LIPS MOVE. IT SPOKE TO ME FROM BENEATH THE WIDE BRIM OF A WORKMAN'S HAT.

"NUMBER FORTY-TWO IS MINE. STAY AWAY FROM THIS PLACE. I'M WATCHING YOU."

AND THEN, ALL AT ONCE, MY OWN VOICE RETURNED. I SCREAMED, I BACKED UP, AND THE OLD WOODEN RAIL FELL AWAY. I REMEMBER NOW LOOKING UP AS I FELL AND SEEING THAT WHATEVER HAD STOOD

49

OVER ME WAS GONE. IT HAD VANISHED. OR HAD IT BEEN THERE AT ALL?

SARAH'S VIDEO OF THE LEG WALKING PAST, DRAGGING THE OTHER BEHIND IT, MAKES ME SURER THAN EVER THAT WHAT I SAW THAT NIGHT WAS REAL. I CAN'T TELL ANYONE BUT SARAH OR THEY'LL PUT ME IN THE LOONY BIN. I FELT LIKE PEOPLE WERE WATCHING ME BEFORE THE ACCIDENT, BUT NOW IT'S MUCH WORSE. MY PARENTS ARE WATCHING ME. I'M CERTAIN THEY'LL HAVE EVERYONE ELSE IN TOWN WATCHING ME. FRIDAY, HENRY WILL ARRIVE AND HE'LL BE WATCHING. GLADYS WITH HER SHOTGUN IS WATCHING ME. THE RAVEN IS WATCHING AT MY WINDOW.

AND THE THING AT THE DREDGE — IT HAS TO BE WATCHING.

WAITING.

OR MAYBE IT'S COMING TO GET ME.

Tuesday, September 14, nearly PM

My leg feels worse tonight. I think it's the stress. There's a deep pain working its way up my back. Besides going to the bathroom, I haven't gotten out of bed all day. But I've calmed down. Writing everything out helped. It seems more like a story now. It feels better.

I'm finding that dull, lingering pain is ten times worse when it's accompanied by dull, lingering boredom. If not for my laptop I'm pretty sure my parents would have already found me dead from a hopeless case of endless monotony.

I can imagine it:

"Our little Ryan has died of boredom. We should have looked in on him more. Poor thing."

So the laptop rests nicely on Big Bertha. My mom says the psychiatrist gave her some software that secretly tracks my browser history, emails, IMs, everything. It's nice that my mom told me this, because the software isn't very hard to disable. Adults in general take a lot of comfort in these tools, but a fifteen-year-old who can't get around parental controls on a

COMPUTER IS PROBABLY ALSO HAVING TROUBLE TYING HIS SHOES. IT'S JUST NOT THAT HARD.

STILL, TIMING IS IMPORTANT. I CAN'T BE SEARCHING FOR WEIRD STUFF OR SENDING EMAILS TO SARAH WITHOUT HAVING AT LEAST A FEW MINUTES TO COVER MY TRACKS. IT TAKES TIME TO ERASE WHAT I'VE DONE, AND IT'S TOO LATE IF I'VE JUST SENT AN EMAIL AND I HEAR MY MOM WALKING UP THE STAIRS.

NOT THAT I'VE SENT SARAH ANY EMAILS. I STILL DON'T KNOW WHAT TO SAY.

IT'S HARD. MAYBE TOO HARD.

TO KILL THE BOREDOM, I'VE BEEN SEARCHING ONLINE FOR INFORMATION ABOUT THE DREDGE. SARAH AND I HAVE LOOKED BEFORE AND FOUND ALMOST NOTHING OF INTEREST. WE SEARCHED FOR ARCHIVED STORIES, BLOGS BY PEOPLE LIVING IN TOWN, INFORMATION ABOUT THE CROSSBONES, THE SKELETON CREEK IRREGULAR, AND A LOT MORE. IN EVERY CASE WE DISCOVERED WHAT FELT LIKE TINY SHARDS OR FRAGMENTS OF INFORMATION, JUST ENOUGH TO KEEP US GOING BUT NOTHING REALLY EARTH-SHATTERING.

I TRIED ALL THOSE ANGLES AGAIN TODAY WITH THE SAME MEAGER RESULTS. AFTER THREE HOURS OF DEAD

52

ENDS, I LOOKED BACK THROUGH MY NOTES AND MY EYES LIT ON THE NAME OF THE COMPANY THAT HAD OWNED THE DREDGE — New York Gold and Silver. I'D SEARCHED THAT TERM BEFORE, BUT NOT VERY AGGRESSIVELY. I WENT LOOKING FOR THEM AGAIN, THIS TIME WITH MORE TENACITY.

New York Gold and Silver HAS BEEN OUT OF BUSINESS FOR OVER TWENTY YEARS, BUT ONE THING ABOUT BANKRUPTCY I'VE FOUND IS THAT ALL YOUR RECORDS ARE OPEN FOR VIEWING. I FOUND A PUBLIC FILE OF THE COMPANY RECORDS IN A SUBSECTION OF THE CITY OF New York LEGAL ARCHIVES, AND WITHIN THOSE FILES I DISCOVERED A FILE MARKED NYGS A M MNS. 80–85. I KNEW NYGS STOOD FOR New York Gold and Silver. WHEN I DOUBLE-CLICKED ON THE FILE, I SAW THAT A M MNS STOOD FOR Annual Meeting Minutes AND THAT 80–85 MEANT 1980–1985.

To CATEGORIZE THIS DOCUMENT AS BORING WOULD BE WAY TOO KIND. THIS WAS 127 PAGES OF PURE, UNDISTILLED DRUDGERY. I SKIMMED THE FIRST 30 PAGES OF PE RATIOS, COST-BENEFIT ANALYSES, PLANT CLOSURES, EQUITY-TO-DEBT RATIOS, SUB-PRIME

HOLDINGS, AND A LOT OF OTHER PAINFULLY TEDIOUS DETAILS OF A ONCE-PROSPEROUS COMPANY. IT WASN'T UNTIL I WAS HALF ASLEEP ON PAGE 31 THAT I REALIZED I COULD SEARCH FOR TERMS I WAS INTERESTED IN RATHER THAN READ EVERY SINGLE WORD.

AND THAT'S WHEN I FOUND SOMETHING ON PAGE 81 AND SOMETHING ELSE ON PAGE 111 THAT MADE ME NERVOUS. I PRINTED THEM OUT, AND I'M GOING TO TAPE THEM IN HERE.

NYGS AM Mins. -- Paragraph 3, page 81.

The #42 asset holding in Skeleton Creek, Oregon, encountered a series of break-ins during the period ending 12-81. Mentioned here due to injuries and subsequent lawsuit brought by local resident Mark Henderson. Claimant asserts he was attacked while searching the #42 dredge on the night of 9-12-81, sustaining injuries to the head and neck, including a major concussion. Lawsuit settled out of court on 11-14-81. Legal department cited private property status in early, low six-figure settlement. No information from local authorities is available on a possible suspect in the attack or if such a suspect exists. #42 asset has been more adequately secured. Consider demolition or removal.

NYGS AM Mins. -- Paragraph 1, page 111.

The #42 asset holding in Skeleton Creek, Oregon, was entered by a private citizen during the period ending 12-84. Three juveniles claim to have visited the dredge repeatedly between 6-84 and 9-84. Court file indicates breaking and entering, destruction of private property, theft of tools, vandalism. One of the three juveniles, Jody Carlisle, claims the three were told not to return by someone they heard but could not see. Legal department strongly advises removal or destruction of asset #42. Approved. Demolition of asset #42 scheduled for 4-11-85.

IN THE SPRING OF 1985, NEW YORK GOLD AND SILVER WAS SERVED WITH ENVIRONMENTAL LAWSUITS FROM OREGON, WASHINGTON, ALASKA, MONTANA, AND IDAHO. I GUESS THEY WERE TOO BUSY FENDING OFF ENEMIES TO TAKE ACTION ON THEIR AGREEMENT TO DEMOLISH #42. BY JUNE OF 1985, THE COMPANY WAS DISSOLVED IN A SEA OF DEBT AND LEGAL DISPUTES. THINGS LIKE THE DREDGE IN SKELETON CREEK WERE FORGOTTEN AS LAWYERS MOVED ON TO

HIGHER-PROFILE CASES. THERE WAS NO MONEY TO
BE MADE SUING A DEAD COMPANY.

IT'S ALMOST NINE O'CLOCK NOW. MOM AND DAD
WILL BE IN TO SAY GOOD NIGHT AND CHECK UP ON ME.
THEY'LL WANT TO CHECK MY COMPUTER.

I KNOW WHAT I HAVE TO DO.

Sarah,

This is going to be really quick — I have to cover my tracks before my mom checks in. I did some digging and found the minutes from some New York Gold and Silver meetings in the 80s. I'm copying you on two paragraphs I found (see below). We're not the first ones to see something weird at the dredge. Every time someone gets close, they get hurt or scared off. Don't go back there. Let's just wait until my parents send me back to school so we can talk without having to be so secretive. That's what — maybe a month? We can figure things out when they can't stop us from seeing each other in the halls.

Another thing — New York Gold and Silver called the dredge the "#42 asset." That night, when you recorded the accident, I heard something. It was a warning, the same as those other kids must have gotten.

"Number forty-two is mine. Stay away from this place. I'm watching you."

And I think I saw him — I think I saw Old Joe Bush. Either that or I'm going crazy.

God, I wish I wasn't writing this as the sun goes down. Write me back — let me know you're okay — but don't do it until tomorrow morning. I'll read and delete.

Don't do anything stupid!

Ryan.

P.S. Henry arrives Friday — keep a lookout for him.

I PASTED THE TEXT FROM THE MEETING NOTES UNDER MY NAME AND PRINTED OUT THE EMAIL (WHICH IS WHAT'S INCLUDED ABOVE).

I HOPE SARAH FINDS MY EMAIL BEFORE HER PARENTS DO.

WEDNESDAY, SEPTEMBER 15, EARLY AM

MOM GAVE ME MORE PAINKILLERS LAST NIGHT — THE KIND WHERE THEY WARN YOU NOT TO OPERATE HEAVY EQUIPMENT AFTER TAKING THEM BECAUSE YOU GET REALLY DROWSY. I FELL ASLEEP READING THE END OF TO A GOD UNKNOWN. STEINBECK COULD BE CREEPY WHEN HE WANTED TO BE, LIKE WHEN JOSEPH WAYNE LIVES ALL ALONE AT THE BLACK ROCK AND LISTENS TO THE SOUNDS OF THE DEEP NIGHT UNTIL IT DRIVES HIM CRAZY. I NEED TO START READING DIFFERENT BOOKS. MAYBE I'LL TRY A ROMANCE NOVEL OR A MEMOIR ABOUT SOMEONE WHO ENJOYED A REALLY HAPPY LIFE.

THE BIG NEWS:

SARAH JUST SENT ME AN EMAIL, WHICH I HAVE READ, PRINTED, AND DELETED.

Ryan,

I'm glad you wrote to me. I was thinking maybe you wouldn't. I would've been okay with that.

It seems like we're doing better detective work apart than we ever did together. You're not the only one making progress. I also found something. I'll send a video and a password tomorrow morning — delete the passwords after you get them. We need to keep all this secure where no one but you and I can access.

You're not writing any of this down, are you? Your parents might read this stuff while you're sleeping — that's exactly the kind of thing parents do when they think their son is up to something. Just try not to write things down all the time, okay?

I listened to the audio track on the video again, and the camera didn't pick up a voice that night. It must have been so quiet only you could hear it. I heard the tapping (makes no sense) but no voice. The #42 reference — maybe it means what we're dealing with is somehow connected to New York Gold and Silver.

It's chilling . . . don't you think? I mean, chilling in a good way. Something really important is going on and we're going to figure it out. Whatever caused you to fall — that spirit or phantom or whatever it is — we have to get to the bottom of it. If it really is a phantom — a real . . . *ghost* — what are we going to do? I have to get more evidence on tape or no one is going to believe us.

That stuff you sent — about the company from New York — I'm not worried about it. Those other people were trying to get money or thrills. What we're doing is different — we're serious, like investigators. I'm being careful and quiet — don't worry about me. I'm fine. Oh, and I asked evil eye outside the bar about Mark Henderson, that guy who sued for money. He's long gone. He left Skeleton Creek right after they gave him the money (figures). The kids weren't named, so I think that's a dead end. I guess we could ask Shotgun Gladys. She makes me nervous.

Check back early tomorrow morning, around 5:30 a.m., before your parents wake up. Make sure to get rid of this stuff — my parents put something on my computer to monitor my activity (I disabled it) — did you check your computer? Some of this new stuff is harder to get around.

How's the leg?

Don't write things down.

XO
— Sarah.

P.S. The fall wilderness ranger arrived last night. He's here from Missoula, probably until everything is snowed in. I might interview him like the ones before. Not sure.

I'D NEVER ASK SARAH TO STOP MAKING MOVIES, SO SHE REALLY SHOULDN'T EXPECT ME TO STOP WRITING. SHE KNOWS I CAN'T STOP. BUT SHE MAKES A GOOD POINT. IF MY PARENTS ARE SNEAKING AROUND IN HERE AFTER I'M ASLEEP, LOOKING FOR MY JOURNALS, I NEED TO MAKE SURE THEY DON'T FIND THEM. I'VE BEEN

PUTTING THIS ONE BETWEEN MY MATTRESS AND THE HEADBOARD SO I CAN PULL IT OUT AND WRITE IN IT WHENEVER I WANT TO. I THINK I'D CATCH THEM IF THEY TRIED TO TAKE IT WHILE I SLEPT. WOULDN'T I?

OH, MAN, THIS REMINDS ME OF <u>THE TELL-TALE HEART.</u> ONLY SIX PAGES, BUT EVERY ONE OF THEM SERIOUSLY SPINE-CHILLING. I CAN IMAGINE MY DAD QUIETLY ENTERING MY ROOM IN THE DARK. HE'S MOVING SO SLOWLY IT TAKES HIM AN HOUR TO GET TO MY BED — JUST LIKE THE MADMAN IN THAT STORY. I HEAR SOMETHING AND SIT UP, BUT IT'S PITCH-BLACK AND I'M AFRAID TO TURN ON THE LIGHT, SO I DON'T SEE HIM STANDING THERE. I SIT UPRIGHT FOR A LONG TIME AND I KNOW SOMEONE IS IN THE ROOM EVEN THOUGH I CAN'T SEE THEM. I'M TERRIFIED. AND THEN <u>BANG!</u> — HE TAKES MY JOURNAL AND ESCAPES.

PERFECT. NOW I HAVE ONE MORE THING TO WORRY ABOUT TONIGHT.

<u>INVESTIGATING</u> IS OFTEN HOW SARAH GETS HERSELF AND ME INTO TROUBLE, SO I'M WORRIED THAT SHE USED THE WORD. AND HER EMAIL HAS THAT BLIND CONFIDENCE SHE GETS SOMETIMES, LIKE SHE'S WEARING GLASSES THAT ONLY LET HER SEE TWO FEET IN FRONT OF HER OWN FACE.

61

Thursday, September 16, early morning

Last night, after dinner, my parents moved me out to the porch so I could get some fresh air. It's getting chilly in the early evening already, but I like that about living in the mountains. The clean air is even crisper when it's chilled. I was exhausted when I finally got back to my room. I fell right to sleep (no doubt the fresh air helped). I got the video and the link from Sarah.

Ryan,

Don't write this down and make sure you delete it and check your tracks. This is SO freaky — we need to talk about it. How? How can we get around your parents?

I'm interviewing the new park ranger with my hidden camera today. Something's not right about him. I saw him at the mart and he wouldn't make eye contact with me. Can't put my finger on it — he's definitely off, like he's trying to hide something. I don't think he knows about what happened at the dredge — or maybe he does. It's on forest service land. Maybe someone told him.

Email me after you watch if you can — my parents are in the house — gotta go.

Sarah.

SARAHFINCHER.COM
PASSWORD:
PITANDPENDULUM

Thursday, September 16, morning

So Sarah thinks my ghost — or whatever it was — was there the first night she went to the dredge. And the dragging leg — that would point to Old Joe Bush, wouldn't it?

It's good that Sarah doesn't think I'm insane.

But that might be because she's insane, too.

Either way, she's good company.

I'm supposed to be the paranoid one. But what is she doing? Driving by my house to make sure I'm okay. Checking the doorway ten times a second to make sure nobody catches her. Asking me not to write anything down.

What's going on?

That might be the worst thing about being trapped in here: I have no idea what's going on outside this room.

I wish I could remember more. I don't think I have amnesia . . . or do I? I remember my name, my age, my address, and my phone number. When my mom comes in my room wearing the

CHILI-PEPPER APRON I GAVE HER WHEN I WAS IN THE EIGHTH GRADE, I RECOGNIZE HER.

I REMEMBER, AT THE AGE OF TEN, HOLDING A COLD MARSHMALLOW MILKSHAKE IN ONE HAND WHILE RIDING MY TEN-SPEED DOWN A HILL. A DOG STARTED CHASING ME AND I SQUEEZED THE FRONT BRAKE. AFTER I FLIPPED OVER THE HANDLEBARS AND LANDED ON MY BACK, I SAT UP AND SAW THAT THE DOG HAD LOST INTEREST IN TRYING TO KILL ME. HE WAS LICKING MY MILKSHAKE OFF THE HOT PAVEMENT.

YOU SEE THERE? I REMEMBER EVERY DETAIL. I REMEMBER EVEN MORE THAN THAT.

I REMEMBER WHEN I LIMPED HOME WITH SKINNED KNEES AND ELBOWS. MY SHIRT WAS ALL DIRTY. MOM WASN'T HOME, SO IT WAS A RARE MOMENT IN WHICH DAD WAS MY LONE HOPE OF SYMPATHY. MOM WOULD HAVE BABIED ME, BUT I RECALL FEELING AS IF I'D BETTER NOT BE CRYING WHEN I REACHED THE PORCH. I KNEW HE WOULDN'T LIKE IT IF I WAS ALL UPSET.

WHEN HE SAW ME, DAD SAT ME ON HIS LAP AND TOUCHED MY STINGING KNEES WITH A COLD DISHRAG FROM THE KITCHEN SINK.

"Mom's not going to like finding blood all over her good rag," I pointed out.

"Don't worry about your mother. I'll cover for you."

That made me smile, even though I was still concerned. "What will you say?"

"Bloody nose. I'll tell her I got in a fight. I'll say someone punched me."

"She's not going to believe you."

"Cutting vegetables?"

"You only cook pancakes."

"You worry too much."

It was a pleasant moment with my dad, like — I don't know — intimate, I guess. It didn't happen very often. He pushed his T-shirt up with a finger and scratched his bare shoulder. I caught sight of a little mark he had.

"What's that?" I asked.

"Tattoo. From a long time ago. You've seen it before."

"Can I see it again?"

He hesitated. I'd only ever seen the tattoo

ABOUT THREE TIMES IN MY WHOLE LIFE. IT WAS SMALL, ABOUT THE SIZE OF A NICKEL. HE CALLED IT HIS LITTLE BIRDIE.

"IT DOESN'T LOOK LIKE A BIRD."

"IT'S NOT A BIRD. I JUST CALL IT THAT."

"WHAT IS IT THEN?"

"IT'S NOTHING."

HE PULLED HIS SLEEVE BACK DOWN AND SET ME ON THE PORCH. THE INTIMATE MOMENT HAD PASSED. I REMEMBER THINKING I'D DONE SOMETHING WRONG.

SO IT SEEMS I REMEMBER A LOT OF THINGS — EVEN LONG STRINGS OF THINGS THAT HAPPENED YEARS AGO. I JUST DON'T RECALL ALL THE DETAILS OF THE NIGHT WHEN I FELL. I GUESS THAT MAKES IT A BLACKOUT, OR IN MY CASE, A GRAY-OUT, SINCE THINGS KEEP CREEPING BACK THAT I DON'T NECESSARILY WANT TO REMEMBER.

I'M NOT SURPRISED BY WHAT SARAH'S SAYING IN THE VIDEO, ABOUT THE SOUND BEING THERE BOTH NIGHTS. IT WAS LIKE I'VE ALREADY SEEN AND HEARD THIS INFORMATION THROUGH A DIRTY WINDOW, AND NOW THE WINDOW HAS BEEN CLEANED. THINGS I ALREADY KNEW HAVE BECOME A LITTLE CLEARER, THAT'S ALL.

67

Thursday, September 16, 11:00 A.M.

I've watched it now a dozen times. No, more than a dozen. And, yes, I might have discovered something. Not just in the visuals. But the sounds. Especially the sounds — over and over and over again with those sounds. The best way I can describe it is that listening to those sounds again and again is like feeling my memory come unstuck from skipping on an old record. The sound of the leg being dragged — dragged — dragged — and then ping! Something clicked forward in my memory. Something that wasn't there before.

I remember it was dark and I wanted to go home. I was looking at the rusted-over gears, trying to imagine how they could have moved. The flashlight felt clammy in my hand when I pointed it to a thick wooden beam that stood behind the machinery. Leaning over the biggest of the many gears, I peered down onto the hidden floorboards below. There was a little round mark, about the size of a nickel. I'd seen that mark before.

The record started skipping again. It's a birdie, it's a birdie, it's a birdie.

What does it all mean?

Sarah,

Your message seems to have nudged my memory. I remember something else from that night that I didn't before. There was a mark or a symbol — I'm not certain what it was — but I saw something carved into one of the wood planks where I stood. It was hidden behind the machinery on the floor. I've drawn a picture and scanned it in so you can see it.

The carving looked like this:

Now, don't get too hysterical, because I have no idea what it means yet, but I'm pretty sure my dad has a tattoo with the same mark. It's the same size and it looks kind of like a bird or an eyeball with some extra junk sticking out.

I'm going to talk with my dad. Don't worry — not about what I saw, not yet at least. I'm just going to ask him about Old Joe Bush and the dredge and see if he tells me anything. My dad could be connected to the dredge somehow — which is really freaking me out — but I don't want to assume anything.

It's also possible I'm imagining what I think I saw. Don't tell anyone this, okay? But sometimes it feels like my mind is playing tricks on me. I was thinking about the birdie, about an old memory I had, then I watched the video like a dozen times in a row and suddenly I remembered seeing the same thing on the dredge that night. Which memory came first? Are they both real or is one of them imagined? I spend a lot of time thinking about things like this. Too much time.

Listen, Sarah, I don't think I'm going to make it unless I turn this into a story. I'm going to crack under all the pressure. I can feel it. So it's a story, right? I'll call it "The Ghost of Old Joe Bush" — that's what it is — a phantom killed by metal and machines on the dredge. I have to give it a name and write it down so it won't scare me so much.

There's a phantom that carries a hammer in one hand and a lantern in the other. Where did the phantom come from? Why is it pounding on the machinery with the hammer? One of its legs is covered in blood and the blood has left a trail. I could follow the trail if I wanted to. It would lead to the bottom of a black lake, to a secret someone is trying to hide.

This could be a very spooky tale if I really put my mind to it. You think?

I'm calling my dad up here to talk with him and then I'm going to write down everything he says. Maybe he'll tell me something because I'm injured. Sometimes he's sympathetic when I'm hurt. I'll have to ask the right questions.

I have a feeling my parents are paying close attention, even more than when I arrived. They keep warning me not to contact you. Don't get in touch with me very often. Only when you have to. Let's just take it slow.

Be careful! — Ryan

P.S. I'm feeling a little better today. I think I'm going to take on the stairs by myself tomorrow and sit outside. The air is starting to catch that chill I like so much in the late afternoon.

Thursday, September 16, 6:00 p.m.

I talked to my dad.

I'll try to get it all down here.

This is just like I heard it. I swear.

I can remember what we said because I knew I'd have to remember it. It was almost like I recorded the conversation so I could write it down after.

I started off by asking him, "Do you remember when I crashed my bike and you cleaned me up?"

He looked at me a little strangely — this wasn't what he was expecting me to say. But he went along with it.

"I remember," he said. "Your mother found the dishrag in the laundry. She asked if I'd killed a gopher."

"You never told me that."

He shrugged. "How's the leg?" he asked.

"It's stiff until afternoon. Then it warms up and it's not so bad."

"Henry gets in tomorrow morning. We'll bring you outside and you can get some fresh air on the porch. You can watch me skewer him at cribbage. How'd that be?"

I NODDED SO HE KNEW I THOUGHT IT WAS A FINE IDEA.

THEN I JUST WENT RIGHT OUT AND ASKED, "DID YOU EVER MEET OLD JOE BUSH?"

HE PAUSED, SITTING AT THE FOOT OF THE BED AS HE LOOKED AT MY CAST. HE GOT UP AND LEFT THE ROOM. I WAS SURE I'D COMPLETELY BLOWN IT. BUT WHEN HE RETURNED, THERE WAS A PICTURE IN HIS HAND. HE HANDED IT TO ME.

"THAT'S OLD JOE BUSH RIGHT THERE."

IT WAS A PICTURE OF A MAN STANDING BEFORE THE GEARS ON THE DREDGE, THE SAME GEARS I HAD STOOD IN FRONT OF ON THE NIGHT OF THE ACCIDENT. THE GEARS WEREN'T RUSTED. THEY WERE BLACK AND GREASY. THE MAN WORE WORK GLOVES AND OVERALLS AND GLASSES. HE WAS A BIG MAN, NOT THE SLIGHTEST BIT PHOTOGENIC. HE HAD THE DAZED LOOK OF SOMEONE WHO HAD BEEN BOTHERED AND WANTED TO BE LEFT ALONE. HAD HE BEEN CAUGHT IN THE MIDDLE OF SOMETHING IMPORTANT?

"HE WORKED ON THE DREDGE, RIGHT?" I ASKED.

MY DAD NODDED ALMOST IMPERCEPTIBLY. "HE GOT CARELESS."

"YOU MEAN HE GOT KILLED?"

He pointed to the picture.

"Those gears pulled him right through and spit him down into the water. They say he drowned because every pocket he had was full of stolen gold. Old Joe Bush sank like his feet were in concrete, right to the bottom."

There was a long silence. My dad walked to the window and looked out, then back at me. And then I felt the sting of why he was talking to me.

"Keep that picture. Let it be a warning. Old Joe Bush got pulled into those gears because he wasn't careful. You nearly died doing something careless yourself. Don't let it happen again."

Even though his message was clear, I figured I might as well ask him something he would probably think was stupid. With my father, moments like this — of true conversation — were pretty few and far between.

"Did Joe Bush ever . . . come back?" I asked.

From the look in his eye, I could see I was going to get an answer. My dad likes a good story, though I've never known him to write one down. He can tell one if one is needed. He likes

THE IDEA OF MYTHS AND SPIRITS. I THINK IT'S PART OF
WHY I WRITE THE THINGS I DO. WE'RE BOTH
STORYTELLERS IN OUR OWN WAY AND I DIDN'T FALL
TOO FAR FROM THE TREE.

"THERE'S A LEGEND THAT USED TO BE TOLD BY
SOME OF THE LAST GUYS WHO WORKED ON THAT
DREDGE," HE SAID. "THEY NEVER TALKED ABOUT IT
OPENLY, ONLY AMONG THEMSELVES. BUT WORD
GETS OUT."

MY DAD ITCHED HIS SHOULDER WHERE THE BIRDIE
LAY HIDDEN UNDER HIS SHIRT.

"THEY SAID THEY COULD HEAR OLD JOE BUSH
WALKING AROUND AT NIGHT, DRAGGING THAT CURSED LEG
OF HIS. THEY COULD HEAR HIM RAPPING ON THE METAL
BEAMS WITH THAT BIG WRENCH HE USED TO CARRY
AROUND TO WORK ON THE GEARS. BIGGEST WRENCH
ANYONE EVER SAW. TAP. TAP. TAP. THEY'D HEAR
IT. THEN IT WOULD STOP. SOMETHING WOULD FALL
MYSTERIOUSLY INTO THE WATER — SOMETHING
IMPORTANT, LIKE A SPECIAL TOOL OR A BOX OF
PARTS — BUT NO ONE WAS GOING DOWN INTO THE
BLACK TO FIND WHAT WENT MISSING. THEY SAID OLD
JOE BUSH HAD WET BOOTS, LIKE HE'D CRAWLED UP

75

OUT OF THE WATER BENEATH THE DREDGE WHERE HE DROWNED AND CAME BACK TO CLAIM WHAT WAS HIS. ONLY HE COULDN'T FIND IT."

"CLAIM WHAT?"

"WHY, ALL THE MISSING GOLD, OF COURSE. WHAT ELSE WOULD HE BE LOOKING FOR?"

MY DAD LAUGHED AND SAID IT WAS ONLY A TALL TALE. THEN HE HEADED FOR THE DOOR.

"HAVE YOU TALKED TO SARAH?" HE ASKED, AND THIS TIME I WAS SURPRISED BY THE SUDDENNESS OF THE QUESTION.

"NO, SIR," I SAID. TECHNICALLY, THIS WAS TRUE. WE HADN'T ACTUALLY TALKED. BUT STILL I WAS NERVOUS — MY DAD HAD FIGURED ME OUT ON LESSER LIES.

"LET'S KEEP IT THAT WAY," HE SAID.

AND THEN HE WAS GONE.

Thursday, September 16, 9:00 p.m.

Henry arrives tomorrow morning from New York. He hasn't visited since last summer, so I'm very interested to talk with him. When Henry visits, he stays in the guest room downstairs. He and my dad are sort of like best friends, I guess. They fly-fish, hike, play cards, and laugh a lot. My dad doesn't usually laugh that much, so it's very noticeable when Henry is around.

I like Henry because, for starters, he's talkative. It can be difficult to make him shut up, if you want to know the truth. I think it has something to do with the fact that everyone else is pretty quiet around here and he's used to more noise in the city. Maybe the sound of his own voice is like the droning background noise he's accustomed to.

Henry wears rainbow-colored suspenders and a crisp white shirt wherever he goes, so you can see the good time coming from a long way off. He has muttonchops — and I don't mean for dinner — really wide. Like, Elvis in the 70s sideburns.

He has a reputation for throwing the most outrageous poker parties in Skeleton Creek during his visits. Playing cards with Henry is a little different than cards with normal people, because there's always an unknown array of punishments for losing hands. You might be forced to wear oven mitts and keep playing. Or you could end up in a full-body wet suit, snorkel, and an underwater mask. And there are the ridiculous wigs, crank calls to wives and girlfriends, blocks of ice that need sitting on, and helium balloons to be inhaled with preposterous scripts to be read in chipmunk voices. A little bit of money changes hands, but mostly everyone hangs around and laughs really, really hard. Even my dad.

Henry's past in Skeleton Creek is complicated. A long time ago, when the dredge was still tearing up the woods, Henry used to visit more often. That's because he was employed by New York Gold and Silver. He was in charge of what I now know were assets number

42, 43, and 44, all dredges scattered around the western states. That meant constant visits in order to assess progress, hire and fire workers, map the movements of the dredges, package and ship the gold, and basically oversee the operation of not one but three dredges. He was young then, a graduate of Georgetown looking to make his mark in the world. He's changed a lot over the years.

I'm hoping he can help me.

Henry was born and raised in the big city, but I think there was something about Skeleton Creek that affected him from the very beginning. It probably happens to a lot of people from New York. They visit Yellowstone Park or Montana or Sun Valley and when they go back home they realize that skyscrapers are not the same as mountains, a hundred taxis are not the same as a hundred cows, and the subway doesn't ride like a horse.

I also think Henry feels guilty about working for a company that tore up the land,

TOOK ALL THE RICHES, AND LEFT SKELETON CREEK HIGH AND DRY. PEOPLE SEEM TO LIKE HIM AROUND HERE — ESPECIALLY MY DAD — AND THERE DON'T SEEM TO BE ANY HARD FEELINGS. I THINK THAT'S BECAUSE HENRY GENUINELY LOVES SKELETON CREEK AND HATES WHAT HAPPENED TO IT. MAYBE HE'S DOING PENANCE FOR THE WORK HE DID IN HIS TWENTIES, BACK WHEN HE DIDN'T KNOW ANY BETTER. HE KEEPS COMING BACK YEAR AFTER YEAR, BURNING UP ALL HIS VACATION TIME ON A DEAD-END TOWN FULL OF DEAD-END PEOPLE. I GUESS THAT COUNTS FOR SOMETHING.

THIS VISIT WILL BE MUCH MORE INTERESTING THAN HENRY'S PAST VISITS. HE STAYS EVERY FALL FOR TWO OR THREE WEEKS DEPENDING ON HOW MUCH VACATION TIME HE HAS SAVED UP. HE COMES FOR THE SEPTEMBER STEELHEAD RUN, FOR THE POKER, FOR THE FRIENDSHIPS. BUT THIS IS THE FIRST FALL WHEN HIS ARRIVAL COINCIDES WITH MY GREAT INTEREST IN THE DREDGE. IN THE PAST I'VE SPENT ALL MY TIME ASKING HIM EITHER ABOUT NEW YORK OR WHAT PUNISHMENTS HE HAS PLANNED FOR POKER NIGHT. I HAVEN'T ASKED

TOO MANY QUESTIONS ABOUT THE DREDGE, AT LEAST IN PART BECAUSE MY DAD HAS ALWAYS ACTED LIKE IT WAS A BAD IDEA WHENEVER I BROUGHT IT UP.

BUT THIS TIME I'M GOING TO GET HENRY ALONE AND REALLY GRILL HIM.

Thursday, September 16, 10:00 p.m.

Sarah has sent me another video already. Two in one day. She's getting way too careless. I saw the email, but I'm going to wait another hour or two before watching the video so my parents are asleep. The videos are hard enough to watch without the added pressure of wondering whether or not my mom or dad are going to knock on my door. I can't erase my tracks that quickly.

I wonder what she wants.

Thursday, September 16, 11:12 p.m.

That was close. I barely hid my journal in time. If I'd been in the middle of a sentence, I probably would've been caught.

My parents are getting too curious. They're in my room all the time, asking a lot of questions. They keep pestering me about Sarah. Have I talked to her? Have I seen her? Did I know she drove by in the middle of the night?

They came in together right after I finished my last entry.

Dad said, "Don't think just because Henry is coming we're not going to be watching you as closely. We want you out of this bed tomorrow, downstairs or on the porch."

Mom said, "You need to start getting more fresh air. Let's do that tomorrow, okay?"

Then Dad said, "Let's have a look at that computer."

It's just dumb luck Sarah hadn't sent me something in the previous hour, and that I'd already scribbled down the password from her previous email (which I'd already deleted). They'd

HAVE SEEN IT BEFORE I DID, BEFORE I COULD ERASE IT. MY NERVES ARE SHOT AND I'M REALLY TIRED. I KEEP HAVING TO STAY UP LATE AND GET UP EARLY SO I CAN WORK WITH SARAH WITHOUT GETTING CAUGHT. I'M NOT SURE HOW MUCH LONGER I WANT TO DO THIS.

BUT I CAN'T IGNORE THE LATEST PASSWORD.

<u>A MONTILLADO</u>

FROM <u>THE CASK OF A MONTILLADO</u> — A TERRIBLE STORY ABOUT DECEPTION AND REVENGE. I'M CERTAIN SHE'S NEVER READ IT. FORTUNADO TRICKED AND CHAINED, THE SLOW BUILDING OF A WALL TO TRAP HIM UNDERGROUND. IT'S A REALLY AWFUL STORY, NOT ONE OF MY FAVORITES. MAYBE IF I TOLD HER THE STORY, SHE'D STOP PICKING SUCH GHASTLY PASSWORDS.

TOMORROW MIGHT GET COMPLICATED. I BETTER WATCH TONIGHT, EVEN THOUGH I CAN BARELY KEEP MY EYES OPEN.

SARAHFINCHER.COM
PASSWORD:
AMONTILLADO

Thursday, September 16, 11:58 p.m.

What was it that Sarah said?

I'm starting to think everything is connected. The secret society, the dredge, New York Gold and Silver, Old Joe Bush — I think it's all somehow linked together.

But that's not all. It's not just some secret society, New York Gold and Silver, and Old Joe Bush. It's Sarah. And me.

And now this new wilderness ranger.

Why did he ask Sarah if we saw anyone at the dredge?

What does he know?

Which is the same thing as asking:

What don't we know?

I have to try to get some sleep.

If I can.

I have this very weird feeling that someone came in my room last night. I woke up but I was too afraid to look around. Plus, it was dark. I couldn't shake the feeling. And then I started wondering if I'd deleted the history after I watched the last video. I reached under my pillow and felt for my journal. It was there. It doesn't seem like it was moved.

It's crazy how paranoid I am.

I've been lying in bed for an hour staring at the picture my dad left me and replaying the warning in my mind.

<u>Old Joe Bush got pulled into those gears because he wasn't careful.</u> You nearly died doing something careless yourself. Don't let it happen again.

After sixty-one minutes of contemplation, I've determined that what my father asked of me was stupid. Carelessness may not be a virtue, but it's unavoidable, especially for someone my age. And besides, super-careful people are really boring. I know a girl at school who won't drink

OUT OF THE WATER FOUNTAIN. SHE WON'T EAT FOOD FROM THE CAFETERIA. SHE HAS A NOTE FOR GYM CLASS THAT ALLOWS HER TO SIT OUT WHENEVER WE DO SOMETHING SHE FEELS IS TOO DANGEROUS. SHE BARELY HAS A PULSE.

OLD JOE BUSH DOESN'T LOOK LIKE THE CARELESS TYPE. IF I HAD TO SAY WHAT HE LOOKS LIKE IN HIS PICTURE, I'D SAY . . . WELL, I GUESS I'D SAY HE LOOKS SINGLE-MINDED. PROBABLY HE WAS PUSHED. FOUL PLAY, THAT'S WHAT KILLED OLD JOE BUSH, NOT CARELESSNESS.

IT WAS REALLY LATE WHEN I WATCHED SARAH'S VIDEO LAST NIGHT. I DREAMT ABOUT IT, SO WHEN I WOKE UP I WASN'T SURE IF I'D WATCHED IT AT ALL. IN MY DREAM, DARYL BONNER THE RANGER AND GLADYS THE LIBRARIAN WERE WALKING IN THE WOODS. GLADYS HAD HER SHOTGUN AND THEN OLD JOE BUSH CAME OUT OF THE BUSHES DRAGGING HIS LEG AND SAID, "NUMBER FORTY-TWO IS MINE. STAY AWAY FROM THIS PLACE. I'M WATCHING YOU." GLADYS FIRED BUCKSHOT INTO THE AIR, AND OLD JOE BUSH TRIED TO RUN AWAY, DRAGGING HIS LEG DOWN THE PATH TOWARD THE DREDGE. GLADYS LAUGHED AND LAUGHED, BUT DARYL BONNER

WENT ON AHEAD AND HELPED OLD JOE BUSH STEP DOWN INTO THE BLACK POND AND DISAPPEAR UNDER THE WATER. IN MY DREAM, THE POND LOOKED LIKE A TAR PIT.

THE THING ABOUT DREAMS IS THAT THEY SOMETIMES MEAN SOMETHING. I HAVE DREAMS ALL THE TIME, BUT I GET THIS FEELING ABOUT CERTAIN DREAMS THAT MAKES ME THINK SOMETHING IMPORTANT IS HIDDEN THERE. THIS WAS ONE OF THOSE DREAMS. THE STICKY GOO OF THE TAR PIT HIDES THINGS. I KNOW IT DOES.

I DON'T THINK GLADYS IS IMPORTANT. I THINK SHE'S JUST IN THERE BECAUSE I'D NEVER GONE THROUGH A DOOR AND FOUND SOMEONE POINTING A SHOTGUN AT ME. SHE'S BEEN APPEARING IN A LOT OF DREAMS SINCE. SHE'S LIKE WALLPAPER. SHE'S JUST THERE.

BUT RANGER BONNER — HE'S NEW — AND HE'S HELPING JOE INTO THE WATER OR THE TAR. WHY DID I CONNECT THE TWO IN MY DREAM? MY UNCONSCIOUS MIND MUST SEE SOMETHING IN THE VIDEO OR THE PICTURE THAT MY WAKING MIND DOESN'T. AN HOUR OF LOOKING AT THE PICTURE MY DAD GAVE ME ISN'T HELPING ME SEE THINGS CLEARER. I'M GOING TO RISK

89

WATCHING SARAH'S VIDEO AGAIN, BUT THIS TIME I'M
GOING TO KEEP THE PICTURE HANDY SO I CAN LOOK AT
IT. IT'S ALMOST 7:30 AND MY MOM USUALLY COMES
IN BETWEEN 7:30 AND 8:00.

I BETTER HURRY.

Friday, September 17, 7:36 a.m.

No sign of mom yet, and I've watched the video again. I scanned the picture of Old Joe Bush and sent it to Sarah. Dangerous move. If her parents open her email before she does, they'll suspect I've sent it. Even though I used an account that doesn't have my name on it and I didn't say hardly anything.

> This is Joe Bush. Familiar?

I didn't put my name at the end. I just attached the photo and sent it.

I think I know why Daryl Bonner and Joe Bush are together in my dream. It's because in real life they look sort of similar. The photo is grainy, but the bone structure, the nose, the forehead — they're similar. <u>Too</u> similar.

What does that even mean?

Friday, September 17, 8:00 a.m.

Mom has been here with my breakfast and gone. It was a miracle she didn't check my computer, because I totally forgot to erase my tracks. It feels like every day I'm a whisper away from losing everything, including my best friend. I totally believe my parents when they say they'll sell the house and move us to the city if they catch me talking to Sarah. If they knew how much we were emailing — all the stuff we were doing — they'd pack the car and have me out of here tonight.

Like Dad said, I have to be careful. I can't be careless when it comes to communicating with Sarah. There's too much at stake.

I've got something weird I want to try — just to see what will happen. It's not the most careful thing in the world, but I can't stop thinking about it.

Here's my plan:

I'll call the ranger station. It's early, so Ranger Bonner probably won't be on the trail

YET. WHEN HE PICKS UP I'LL ASK FOR JOE BUSH AND SEE WHAT HE SAYS. I WONDER WHAT HE'LL DO? WHAT IF HE HAS CALLER ID? DO RANGER STATIONS HAVE STUFF LIKE THAT?

I'M RISKING IT. IF I GET CAUGHT, I'LL SAY IT WAS A PRANK. I'LL PLAY UP THE FACT THAT I'M CRAZY.

Friday, September 17, 8:10 a.m.

I called Daryl Bonner.

Here's what happened:

Him: "Skeleton Creek Ranger Station."

Me: "Can I speak to Joe Bush?"

Him: "Who is this? Why are you asking for Joe Bush?"

I didn't reply.

Him: "Did Sarah Fincher put you up to this?"

I didn't reply.

Him: "Answer me! Why are you asking about Joe Bush?"

I hung up.

And now I wonder:

Why was he so freaked out?

94

Friday, September 17, 9:15 a.m.

I have just endured an eventful hour and five minutes. About two minutes after I hung up, the phone rang. I tried to intercept the call myself, but I picked up at the same moment my dad did. He's a notoriously quick grabber of the phone. He hates hearing it ring and ring. I thought he'd already be halfway out the door for work, but I guess he stayed late this morning.

Just my luck.

Dad: "Hello."

Bonner: "This is Daryl Bonner at the ranger station. Did you just call this number?"

Dad: "I did not. My son might have."

Bonner: "Is this the home of the boy who had the accident at the dredge?"

Dad: "Might be."

Bonner: "I think he might be getting bored. He just called here with — I don't know — I guess you'd call it a prank call. He asked for Joe Bush, whoever that is. And the girl involved in that accident — Sarah Fincher — she seems

INTERESTED IN THE DREDGE AS WELL. IT MIGHT BE A GOOD TIME TO KEEP AN ESPECIALLY CLOSE EYE ON THEM BOTH. THE DREDGE ISN'T SAFE — AT LEAST THAT'S WHAT THE STATE SUPERVISOR TOLD ME. NO ONE SHOULD BE GOING OUT THERE."

DAD: "I'LL HAVE A TALK WITH MY SON."

BONNER: "THANK YOU."

I HUNG UP RIGHT AFTER THEY DID, THEN LISTENED TO MY DAD COMING UP THE STAIRS AND WONDERED IF MY ACTIONS QUALIFIED AS MORE THAN CARELESS. I HAD THE FEELING THEY DID. SARAH'S INTERVIEW RAN THROUGH MY HEAD, THEN MY CALL. I FELT STUPID FOR HAVING DONE IT. THERE WERE DOTS THAT COULD BE CONNECTED. SARAH, BONNER, ME. THERE WAS A FLURRY OF ACTIVITY. MAYBE IT WAS ENOUGH TO GET THE HOUSE ON THE MARKET.

I ALREADY HAD A FONDNESS FOR HENRY, BUT WHEN THE DOORBELL RANG AND MY DAD WENT BACK DOWNSTAIRS I LIKED HENRY TEN TIMES MORE. OUR FALL VISITOR HAD ARRIVED, AND I WAS SPARED MY DAD'S WRATH. HIS ANGER USUALLY BOILED OVER PRETTY FAST. IF I COULD STAY OUT OF HIS CROSSHAIRS WHILE HE

CALMED DOWN, THE CONSEQUENCES WERE ALWAYS LESS SEVERE. UNTIL HE SHOWED UP IN MY ROOM WITH HENRY IN TOW, I EVEN HAD A GLIMMER OF HOPE THAT MY DAD HAD FORGOTTEN ALL ABOUT THE PHONE CALL.

"THAT'S ONE HECKUVA CAST!"

THOSE WERE THE FIRST WORDS OUT OF HENRY'S MOUTH WHEN HE CAME INTO MY ROOM WITH MY DAD. THEY WERE BOTH SMILING AND I BREATHED A SIGH OF RELIEF.

HENRY WENT ON, "ANY CHANCE I COULD HAVE IT WHEN YOU'RE DONE? THAT THING COULD BE A REAL HIT AT THE CARD TABLE."

"THEY'LL HAVE TO CUT IT OFF. I COULD ONLY GIVE YOU THE PIECES."

"I'VE GOT DUCT TAPE. IT'LL BE PERFECT."

HENRY HAD HIS FISHING HAT ON, RIMMED WITH FLIES, AND HIS RAINBOW SUSPENDERS.

"YOUR DAD TELLS ME HE NEEDS TO RUN ACROSS TOWN AND SEE THE RANGER. MIND IF I KEEP YOU COMPANY WHILE HE'S GONE?"

"I'D LIKE THAT."

MY DAD ASKED FOR HIS PICTURE OF OLD JOE BUSH, AND I GAVE IT TO HIM. HE LOOKED AT ME AS IF

TO SAY, <u>WE'RE NOT QUITE THROUGH HERE YET, I'LL BE BACK</u>, AND THEN HE LEFT ME AND HENRY ALONE IN MY ROOM. I <u>SO</u> WISH I'D NEVER MADE THAT PHONE CALL. IT FEELS LIKE I'VE OPENED A CAN OF WORMS AND THEY'RE SQUIRMING OUT ALL OVER THE PLACE.

HENRY CHIMED IN WHEN THE SOUND OF OUR FRONT DOOR CLOSING REACHED MY ROOM.

"CAN YOU GET DOWN THOSE STAIRS?" HE ASKED.

"I THINK I CAN. BUT I ALWAYS FEEL BETTER IN THE AFTERNOON. I THINK I'LL WAIT A LITTLE BIT."

"FAIR ENOUGH. HOW BORED ARE YOU?"

"VERY."

"I SUSPECTED."

"HOW LONG ARE YOU STAYING?"

"SEVENTEEN DAYS OF BLISS! TWO POKER NIGHTS, FISHING ON THE RIVER, AND YOUR MOM'S HOME COOKING. YOU DON'T APPRECIATE IT NOW, BUT CYNTHIA IS THE QUEEN OF COMFORT FOOD. OLD BACHELORS LOVE COMFORT FOOD, ESPECIALLY WHEN WE'RE FROM THE CITY. SHE'S MAKING THAT BAKED NOODLE DISH WITH THE CRUNCHY CHEESE ON TOP TONIGHT. I'VE BEEN THINKING ABOUT IT FOR THREE DAYS."

"YOU SHOULD GET MARRIED," I JOKED.

"AND GIVE UP YANKEE GAMES, DIRTY LAUNDRY, AND MY TWELVE GIRLFRIENDS? I DON'T THINK I'M READY FOR THAT KIND OF SACRIFICE."

"YOU DON'T HAVE TWELVE GIRLFRIENDS."

"DO SO."

"LIAR."

"WELL, I'VE HAD TWELVE GIRLFRIENDS. IT'S THE SAME THING."

"I BET ALL TWELVE ARE NOW MARRIED WITH KIDS AND HAVE LONG SINCE FORGOTTEN THE YANKEE-LOVING SLOB THEY DATED TEN YEARS AGO."

"YOU SHOULDN'T TALK LIKE THAT WITH A CAST ON YOUR LEG. YOU WON'T BE ABLE TO RUN AWAY WHEN I DUMP A BUCKET OF COLD WATER ON YOUR HEAD."

"YOU'RE ALL TALK."

"I'M MAKING YOUR LUNCH."

HENRY SMILED AND I KNEW I WAS IN BIG TROUBLE. I HATED NOT KNOWING WHAT DISGUSTING THING HE MIGHT ADD TO A HOT POCKET OR SWIRL INTO PEANUT BUTTER BEFORE SPREADING IT AROUND. HE PROBABLY WOULDN'T DO ANYTHING, BUT I'D NEVER KNOW FOR SURE, AND IT WOULD DRIVE ME CRAZY.

WE TALKED ABOUT THE ACCIDENT AND ABOUT HOW I

COULDN'T SEE SARAH ANYMORE. THE NEWS ABOUT SARAH BOTHERED HIM AND HE SAID HE WOULD TALK TO MY PARENTS. HE LIKED SARAH AND I APPRECIATED IT, BUT I KNEW SOMEWHERE DEEP DOWN THAT IT DIDN'T MATTER WHAT HENRY SAID. MY PARENTS HAD ALREADY MADE UP THEIR MINDS.

I HAD NO IDEA HOW MANY MORE TIMES I'D HAVE HENRY TO MYSELF. I DECIDED IT WAS TIME TO BEGIN MY INQUISITION, ESPECIALLY SINCE HE WAS IN SUCH A FRIENDLY MOOD.

"HEY," I SAID. "HOW COME YOU NEVER TALK ABOUT WHEN YOU USED TO WORK FOR NEW YORK GOLD AND SILVER?"

"IT'S NOT MY BEST CHAPTER."

"WHY NOT?"

HENRY TOOK OFF HIS HAT AND LAUGHED NERVOUSLY. THEN HIS SMILE WENT AWAY AND I FELT TERRIBLE FOR ASKING HIM.

"SINCE YOU'RE ALL BUSTED UP, I SUPPOSE I'LL TELL YOU. I MADE A LOT OF MISTAKES BACK THEN BECAUSE I WAS YOUNG AND AMBITIOUS. I COULD LIE AND SAY I DIDN'T REALLY KNOW WHAT I WAS DOING, BUT I KNEW.

Skeleton Creek got into my bones, though. It saved me."

"Did you ever meet Joe Bush?"

Henry looked at me a little curiously then, but he still answered. "Why sure I did — lots of times. He was a hard worker. You know he died on the dredge?"

"I do."

"That accident was the beginning of the end. I quit not too long after that. There were a lot of lawsuits flying around. They were asking me to do things I couldn't do."

"Like what?"

"You sure are curious when you're laid up."

"Like what, Henry?"

"They wanted me to lie about things, and that's when I knew for sure I'd been doing something wrong all along."

"Did you ever hear of Old Joe Bush coming back?"

"You mean like a ghost?"

"I guess so."

"Let's just say there are stories floating around — none of them true, mind you — about the ghost of Old Joe Bush. It's all hogwash."

"Can I ask you one more thing?"

"Sure you can."

"Have you ever heard of the Crossbones?"

"Now there's an interesting question!"

"Really?"

"It's especially interesting for an outsider like me. Did you know membership is only allowed if you can prove you were either born here or have a relative that was born here?"

"No. I didn't know that."

"That's the truth — or at least I think it is. I'm pretty sure the Crossbones came into existence back when the dredge was still working."

"Why do you say that?"

"There was talk of a secret group forming. You hear things."

"What did they do?"

"If I knew that, I'd be a member. But as I said, I'm from the outside. A New Yorker, no less! No

MATTER HOW MUCH I LOVE THIS PLACE OR HOW MANY
TIMES I COME BACK, I'LL NEVER KNOW MORE THAN I DO
RIGHT NOW ABOUT THE CROSSBONES. WHICH ISN'T
MUCH."

I WAS AFRAID TO ASK ONE LAST QUESTION, BUT I
ASKED ANYWAY.

"IS MY DAD A MEMBER?"

"IF I WERE A BETTING MAN, I'D PUT GOOD MONEY ON
IT. BUT THE TRUTH IS, I HAVE NO IDEA. WE TALK ABOUT
A LOT, BUT NOT ABOUT THOSE KINDS OF THINGS."

THEN HE LEFT TO UNPACK HIS THINGS, AND I WROTE
ALL OF THIS DOWN.

I CAN'T WAIT TO TELL SARAH.

BUT HOW?

IT'S RISKIER WITH SOMEONE ELSE AROUND. I DON'T
THINK HENRY WOULD TELL MY PARENTS IF HE CAUGHT
ME EMAILING — BUT I CAN'T BE SURE.

Friday, September 17, 11:00am

When Dad came back, the steam had gone out of his anger and he didn't say a lot about the call I'd made. He didn't give me back the picture of Joe Bush and I didn't ask for it.

"I know you're bored," he said, "but leave that poor man alone. He's new in town and he's got work to do like the rest of us. Find something productive to do."

Like the <u>rest</u> of us? I don't know what he's talking about. My dad is on vacation for the next two weeks while my mom keeps working at the post office like she always does. Henry and my dad will sleep late, make pancakes and strong coffee, then fish and play cards.

I keep wondering how my dad would feel if someone told him he couldn't see Henry ever again. I'm pretty sure he'd go down fighting.

The two of them are downstairs going through their fly boxes, comparing gear, getting ready to go fishing on the river for the afternoon. Skeleton Creek drains into a bigger creek, and that bigger creek drains into the

104

RIVER, WHERE THEY'LL SEARCH OUT WINTER-RUN STEELHEAD (BASICALLY A GIANT TROUT). THE PLACE THEY'RE GOING TO IS AN HOUR OUTSIDE OF TOWN IF MY DAD IS DRIVING THE OLD PICKUP. HE HAS TO BABY IT OR THEY'D BE THERE IN HALF THE TIME.

WHEN DAD AND HENRY GET BACK THEY'LL THROW TOGETHER A LATE LUNCH AND HELP ME DOWN TO THE PORCH AND WE CAN PLAY CARDS BEFORE MOM GETS HOME.

WHAT DID MY DAD SAY TO RANGER BONNER? HE MIGHT NOT HAVE EVEN SEEN THE RANGER. MAYBE HE ONLY SAID HE WAS GOING TO SEE RANGER BONNER AND ACTUALLY WENT TO TALK WITH SARAH'S PARENTS OR, WORSE, A REAL ESTATE AGENT. THERE COULD BE A SIGN GOING UP IN THE FRONT YARD ALREADY.

I DESPISE ALL REAL ESTATE AGENTS.

Friday, September 17, 11:40 a.m.

They left here fifteen minutes ago and I drifted off to sleep. At first I thought there was a phone ringing in my dream, but it kept ringing, and on the fourth ring I reached out my arm and fumbled for the cordless. I expected it to be Mom checking on me. She has a way of knowing when I'm home alone. She tells me to rest, eat, and stay off the Internet.

I clicked on the receiver and answered groggily, hoping she'd hear the fatigue in my voice and go easy on me with the lecturing. When I answered, there was the faintest sound of — what was it? — leaves moving in the trees? Or was it water moving? It had the distinct but indefinable sound of nature. At least that's what I thought before whoever it was hung up on me.

My first thought was that my dad was calling from the stream to make sure I was staying put. But why did he hang up? I looked at the caller ID and didn't recognize the number. It was a 406 area code. Not local.

I dialed the number and waited. One ring. Two rings. Three rings. Voice mail.

"This is Daryl Bonner with the Montana Department of Fish and Wildlife. I'm currently stationed in Skeleton Creek, Oregon, returning to the Wind River Station on November third. Please leave a message."

Why is Ranger Bonner calling my house and then hanging up? Was he looking for my dad and got me instead?

I shouldn't have called him and asked if Old Joe Bush was there.

What if he thinks I know something I'm not supposed to?

THE LAST COUPLE OF HOURS SCOURING THE WEB ANYTHING ABOUT SKELETON CREEK, THE DREDGE, OLD JOE BUSH. I'M SO FRUSTRATED. IT'S LIKE I'VE DUG UP ALL THE BONES I'M GOING TO FIND AND THEY MAKE UP ONLY ABOUT A TENTH OF WHAT I'M SEARCHING FOR. THE DEEPER I GO, THE HARDER THE GROUND FEELS. I FEEL LIKE I'VE HIT A LAYER OF SOLID ROCK.

I NEED TO SEND A WARNING TO SARAH, BUT I'M AFRAID TO. WHAT IF MY DAD WENT TO HER PARENTS AND THEY'VE TAKEN HER COMPUTER? I CAN SEE THEM SITTING AT THE KITCHEN TABLE HITTING REFRESH EVERY FIFTEEN MINUTES WAITING FOR MY EMAIL TO COME THROUGH. THE DEATH EMAIL. THE EMAIL THAT SENDS ME PACKING.

I CAN'T RISK IT.

FRIDAY, SEPTEMBER 17, 1:25 P.M.

OBVIOUSLY SARAH DOESN'T FEEL AS CONCERNED AS I
DO, BECAUSE I JUST GOT AN EMAIL FROM HER. I GUESS
THAT PUTS TO REST MY CONCERN ABOUT HER PARENTS
CONFISCATING HER LAPTOP. UNLESS — AND THIS IS
ENTIRELY POSSIBLE — THEY'RE BAITING ME. WHAT IF
THEY SENT THE EMAIL? OR, WORSE, WHAT IF MY DAD
IS ON SARAH'S LAPTOP AT HER HOUSE WITH HER
PARENTS SENDING ME EMAILS? IT'S AN UNDERHANDED
MOVE, BUT IT COULD HAPPEN.

I'D LIKE TO THINK HENRY WOULD TIP ME OFF. BUT
HOW COULD HE?

I'M HUNGRY AND TIRED, WHICH SOMETIMES MAKES ME
NERVOUS. BUT SERIOUSLY — I AM SO PARANOID. IT'S
RIDICULOUS. MAYBE I NEED GROUP THERAPY. ME,
SARAH, AND OLD JOE BUSH.

ACTUALLY, TO BE FAIR, WHAT I GOT FROM
SARAH WASN'T REALLY AN EMAIL IF YOU CONSIDER
THERE WERE NO WORDS IN THE MESSAGE, ONLY A
STRING OF LETTERS IN THE SUBJECT LINE AND
NOTHING ELSE.

drjekyllandmrhyde

So now she's diverging from Poe into Stevenson. Fair enough. I sometimes think she's trying to tell me something with these passwords. Like in this case, is she saying that Daryl Bonner is Dr. Jekyll, and the ghost of Joe Bush is Mr. Hyde? Or is Daryl Bonner both?

Or is my dad both?

I can't believe I just wrote that. I might as well be Jekyll and Hyde, I keep going back and forth.

I have to get out of this house.

Dad and Henry could come back early. I haven't covered the tracks of my two hours of searching online. I haven't deleted Sarah's email or watched the video. There's a lot to do while I have the house to myself.

I'm getting rid of everything first. Then, if I'm still safe, I'll watch the video.

SARAHFINCHER.COM
PASSWORD:
DRJEKYLLANDMRHYDE

Friday, September 17, 1:52 p.m.

I should have watched the video first! Why am I even writing this? Because it calms me down. That's why I'm writing. It calms me down. I think better when I write.

I can figure this out if I settle down.

Recap:

Sarah went to the dredge.

Ranger Bonner was there. Sarah thinks he was waiting for her. But she could just be overreacting.

She borrowed his phone. She dialed the last number in his incoming calls list.

It was my house. And it was after Dad had already gone over to talk to Bonner. Supposedly. And when I called back? He must have had the ringer silenced in case it went off while he was tailing Sarah through the woods. For once I'm glad there are cell towers scattered out there — at least she could get a signal and call me, even if she couldn't say anything.

Sarah thinks Dad tipped Bonner off. But how could he know she'd be there?

WAS HE IN MY ROOM LAST NIGHT? HAS HE READ THIS? HE COULD HAVE SNUCK IN HERE JUST LIKE THAT CRAZY NUT JOB IN <u>THE TELL-TALE HEART.</u> I WOKE UP — IT FELT LIKE SOMEONE WAS IN THE ROOM, BUT THERE WAS NO ONE. OR AT LEAST NO ONE ANSWERED IN THE DARK.

IF MY DAD KNOWS, THEN WHY ISN'T HE CONFRONTING ME? WHY ISN'T THE HOUSE UP FOR SALE? WHY ISN'T MY MOM FREAKING OUT? SHE'S NOT, SO THAT MEANS HE HASN'T TOLD HER.

HOW MANY QUESTIONS IS THAT — FIFTY? I CAN'T ANSWER ANY OF THEM FOR SURE. I NEED MORE INFORMATION. I NEED TO NARROW THIS DOWN.

WHAT'S THE MOST IMPORTANT QUESTION RIGHT NOW? DAD. WHAT'S GOING ON WITH DAD?

TWENTY MINUTES TOPS, MAYBE FIFTEEN. I CAN'T RISK SNEAKING AROUND BEYOND THAT. THEY'LL STOP FISHING WHEN HENRY GETS HUNGRY. HENRY LIKES TO EAT. HE'LL WANT TO KNOCK OFF EARLY. I BET THEY'LL BE HERE BY 2:30, MAYBE EVEN EARLIER.

I'M JUST GOING TO TAKE MY JOURNAL WITH ME — THAT'S WHAT I'M GOING TO DO. I'LL KEEP WRITING. I'LL HOBBLE TO MY PARENTS' ROOM, RIGHT DOWN THE HALL.

I CAN MAKE THAT WORK. I'LL GO IN THERE. I KNOW
WHERE MY DAD'S DRESSER IS. I KNOW HE KEEPS HIS
PERSONAL STUFF IN THE TOP DRAWER BECAUSE MOM
TOLD ME WHEN I WAS LITTLE. SHE CAUGHT ME IN THERE
AND SLAPPED MY HAND REALLY HARD AND SAID I SHOULD
NEVER SEARCH THROUGH OTHER PEOPLE'S THINGS
WITHOUT ASKING. SHE SAID IT WAS THE SAME AS
STEALING, WHICH I NEVER REALLY UNDERSTOOD.

I'M IN THE DOOR. MY WATCH SAYS 2:03 BUT I'M
LEAVING THE DOOR OPEN SO I CAN HEAR IT IF THEY
COME IN. HENRY WILL BE LOUD — HE'LL BE TALKING.
I'LL BE ABLE TO GET OUT.

MY PARENTS' CLOSET SMELLS LIKE MY MOM, NOT
LIKE MY DAD. I'M HAVING SOME TROUBLE BREATHING. I
JUST CAN'T SEEM TO CALM DOWN. I REMEMBER WHEN
SHE SLAPPED MY HAND AND HOW IT STUNG. THE BLOOD
IS RUSHING THROUGH MY LEG AND I CAN FEEL EVERY
PART THAT'S BROKEN. IT FEELS LIKE MY MOM TOOK A
BROOMSTICK AND STARTED BEATING ME WITH IT.
WHACK! WHACK! WHACK!

I'VE GOT THIS JOURNAL OPEN ON THE TOP OF THE
DRESSER. THE LIGHTBULB DOESN'T MAKE IT VERY
BRIGHT IN HERE. IT'S SORT OF A YELLOW LIGHT. OH,

MAN, I CAN'T BREATHE VERY WELL. DO I HAVE ASTHMA? I MIGHT HAVE ASTHMA, THE MORE I THINK ABOUT IT. I'VE KICKED UP SOME DUST IN HERE. MY LEG IS KILLING ME. IT DOESN'T LIKE BEING STOOD UP FOR TOO LONG ALL AT ONCE.

I KNOW IT'S CRAZY FOR ME TO BE WRITING AS I DO THIS. BUT I HAVE TO.

I MIGHT NOT GET ANOTHER CHANCE TO DO THIS. AND I CAN'T RELY ON MY MEMORY. I HAVE TO GET EVERYTHING DOWN.

THE DRAWER IS OPEN. THERE'S LOTS OF STUFF IN HERE. MY GRANDFATHER'S BELT BUCKLE — HE'S DEAD NOW. IT'S GOT RHINESTONES IN IT. A STACK OF DOCUMENTS — LEGAL STUFF, I THINK. A CIGAR BOX WITH A LITTLE LATCH ON IT. SOME RINGS AND PENS AND OLD WATCHES.

I'VE OPENED THE CIGAR BOX. IT'S GOT A ROW OF TEN OR TWELVE MATCHING CUFF LINKS PUSHED INTO A SHEET OF CARDBOARD. MY DAD NEVER WEARS CUFF LINKS. THERE'S A CAMPAIGN BUTTON, A STACK OF EXPIRED CREDIT CARDS AND LICENSES. THERE'S NOTHING OMINOUS HERE. THERE'S NO SIGN OF A SECRET SOCIETY.

2:12. I HAVE TO GET OUT OF HERE.

WHY CUFF LINKS? I BET THEY'RE FROM THEIR
WEDDING DAY — MAYBE IT'S ALL THE CUFF LINKS FROM
ALL THE MEN IN THE WEDDING PARTY. THEY ALL LOOK
ALIKE, AS IF THEY WERE WORN ONCE AND NEVER AGAIN.

2:13.

I TRIED TO PICK UP ONE OF THE CUFF LINKS, AND
THE WHOLE PIECE OF CARDBOARD LIFTED UP OUT OF THE
CIGAR BOX. WHEN I FLIPPED IT OVER, I FOUND A PIECE
OF PAPER TAPED TO THE BACK. I UNFOLDED IT AND
FOUND SOMETHING THERE. I CAN'T BREATHE. I REALLY
HAVE TO GET OUT OF HERE.

2:15.

THEY'RE GOING TO BE BACK ANY SECOND NOW. I
CAN FEEL IT. I'VE SHUFFLED BACK DOWN THE HALL TO
MY ROOM, DRAGGING MY LEG BEHIND ME. MY
COMPUTER IS SCANNING THE PIECE OF PAPER WHILE I
WRITE. COME ON — FINISH!

2:18.

THE SCAN IS DONE. TIME TO RETURN THE
ORIGINAL.

2:20.

THEY'RE HOME! HENRY JUST YELLED UP THE
STAIRS.

"I'M MAKING LUNCH, CHAMP! I HOPE YOU'RE READY FOR A SURPRISE!"

I'M STANDING IN FRONT OF MY DAD'S DRESSER WITH THE LITTLE YELLOW LIGHT ON. I CAN'T MOVE. HE'LL COME UP HERE ANY SECOND, I KNOW HE WILL. THEN WHAT WILL I DO? I SHOULD RUN. I SHOULD GET OUT OF HERE. I'VE CLOSED THE DRAWER BUT I CAN'T MOVE.

WHAT AM I GOING TO DO?

HE'S COMING.

Friday, September 17, 2:41 p.m.

I've calmed down now. I'm not shaking so much anymore. I can breathe again. My dad went straight to the hallway bathroom on his way to my room. I heard him yell.

"Just going to use the head and I'll stop in and see you. Fishing was good! Better than last year."

I made it out of his room, into the hallway outside the bathroom door. I tucked this journal in the top of my cast and sucked in my breath. The door opened with a whoosh of air.

"Look at you! Up and walking around. You must really want to play some cards."

He looked happy to see me. I felt guilty about that. What was I doing?

"Count me in," I told him. "I'm tired of lying down."

"Looks like you just ran a marathon. How about lunch in bed, then we'll help you to the porch? Deal?"

"Deal."

AND SO DAD DELIVERED ME BACK TO MY ROOM, AND THEN HENRY BROUGHT IN A GRILLED-CHEESE-AND-BACON SANDWICH WITH TOMATO SOUP. IT WOULD BE EASY TO HIDE ALL SORTS OF GROSS THINGS IN CREAMY RED SOUP OR MELTED ORANGE CHEESE. BUT IT WAS LATE AND I WAS STARVING. HE WOULDN'T DARE TRICK A KID WITH A CAST. WOULD HE?

FRIDAY, SEPTEMBER 17, 2:41 P.M.

DAD AND HENRY WILL BE UP TO GET ME ANY MINUTE. I PRINTED OUT THE SCAN OF WHAT I FOUND. I'M STICKING IT TO THIS PAGE. IT SCARES ME.

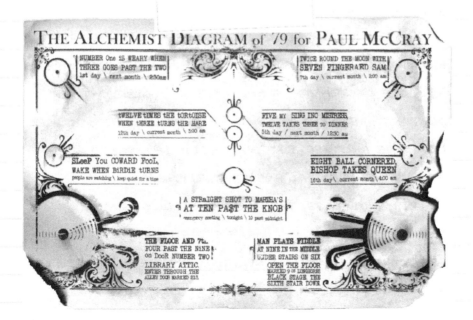

THE ALCHEMIST DIAGRAM of 79 for PAUL McCRAY

NUMBER One IS WEARY WHEN THREE GOES PAST THE TWO
1st day \ next month \ 2:30 am

TWICE ROUND THE MOON WITH SEVEN FINGERARD SAM
7th day \ current month \ 2:00 am

TWELVE TIMES THE TORTOISE WHEN THREE TURNS THE HARE
12th day \ current month \ 3:00 am

FIVE MY SING INC MISTRESS, TWELVE TAKES THREE TO DINNER
5th day / next month / 12:30 am

SLEEP You COWARD FOOL, WAKE WHEN BIRDIE TURNS
people are watching \ keep quiet for a time

EIGHT BALL CORNERED, BISHOP TAKES QUEEN
16th day \ current month \ 4:00 am

A STRAIGHT SHOT TO MARTHA'S AT TEN PAST THE KNOB
emergency meeting \ tonight \ 10 past midnight

THE FLOOR AND 7th. FOUR PAST THE NINE ON DOOR NUMBER TWO
LIBRARY ATTIC.
ENTER THROUGH THE ALLEY DOOR MARKED 923.

MAN PLAYS FIDDLE AT NINE IN THE MIDDLE. UNDER STAIRS ON SIX OPEN THE FLOOR
MARKED 9 or LONGHORNE
BLACK STAGE. THE SIXTH STAIR DOWN

FRIDAY, SEPTEMBER 17, 7:30 P.M.

THERE'S NO TWO WAYS ABOUT IT: NAVIGATING STAIRS IS COMPLICATED WITH A FULL-LEG CAST AND CRUTCHES. OUR STAIRWELL IS NARROW AND THERE ARE FAMILY PICTURES HANGING LIKE CLUMPS OF GRAPES ALL THE WAY DOWN BOTH SIDES. I THINK I WOULD HAVE BEEN FINE IF I HADN'T INSISTED I COULD DO IT ALONE. HENRY AND DAD WERE WATCHING FROM THE BOTTOM OF THE STAIRS WHEN I PITCHED FORWARD SOMEWHERE NEAR THE MIDDLE AND LOST MY BALANCE.

DAD MET ME WITH OUTSTRETCHED ARMS, AND MY FACE SMASHED INTO HIS GRAY T-SHIRT. HE SMELLED LIKE A FISHERMAN.

MY HANDS FANNED OVER ABOUT A DOZEN FAMILY PICTURES IN FRAMES ON THE WAY DOWN BUT BY SOME MIRACLE OF GRAVITY NONE OF THEM FELL TO THEIR DEATHS. THEY WOBBLED BACK AND FORTH AND KNOCKED INTO ONE ANOTHER, BUT THEY HELD. IT LOOKED LIKE A BIG GUST OF WIND HAD RUSHED THROUGH.

IN MY DEFENSE, THE CAST IS REALLY HEAVY AND . . . LET'S SEE . . . WHAT'S THE WORD I'M SEARCHING FOR? . . . UNBENDING. A CAST LIKE BIG

BERTHA MAKES A PERSON WANT TO BEND LIKE NEVER BEFORE. I'M <u>DYING</u> TO BEND MY LEG. IT'S LIKE A FEROCIOUS ITCH I CAN'T SCRATCH. (WHICH REMINDS ME: THIS THING ITCHES LIKE MAD, SO ADD THAT TO MY LIST OF COMPLAINTS.)

WHEN I FINALLY MADE IT TO THE FRONT PORCH, THE FLOORBOARDS CREAKED UNDER THE WEIGHT OF MY CAST. I SETTLED DOWN ON A GOLD, TATTERED COUCH WITH MY LEG PROPPED UP ON A WOODEN STOOL AND BREATHED IN THE CRISP FALL AIR.

OUR PORCH IS A LOT LIKE AN OUTDOOR LIVING ROOM. WHEN A PIECE OF FURNITURE IS REPLACED INSIDE THE HOUSE, THE OLD ITEM FINDS A HOME ON THE PORCH. AFTER A WHILE — A YEAR, MAYBE TWO — THE SAME ITEM MOVES TEN MORE FEET AND BECOMES AN ITEM IN ONE OF MOM'S MANY YARD SALES. IT'S A NATURAL PROGRESSION, A SLOW BUT STEADY MARCH OFF THE PROPERTY.

I SEARCHED THE SKIES FOR FLYING DR PEPPER CANS OR OTHER SIGNS OF SARAH, BUT THERE WAS NOTHING. HENRY ASKED IF I WANTED TO PLAY THREE-HANDED CRIBBAGE. NOT A GREAT GAME IF YOU ASK ME. I'M NOT SURE WHO CAME UP WITH IT, BUT PROBABLY IT WAS THREE PEOPLE SITTING IN A ROOM WITH ONE

CRIBBAGE BOARD AND THE PERSON SITTING OUT WANTED TO JOIN IN. I PLAYED ANYWAY. IT WAS NICE TO THINK ABOUT SOMETHING OTHER THAN HAUNTED DREDGES AND SECRET SOCIETIES.

"HOW MUCH LONGER?" HENRY ASKED AFTER A LITTLE WHILE. HE WAS HOLDING HIS CARDS WITH ONE HAND AND TUGGING SLOWLY ON ONE RAINBOW SUSPENDER WITH THE OTHER.

"BEFORE WHAT?"

"BEFORE YOU CAN WALK AROUND WITHOUT SOMETHING ON YOUR LEG?"

"HOW LONG, DAD?"

.- .-. . | -.-- --- ..- | - .... . | .- .-.. -.-. .... . -- .. ... - |

HENRY COULDN'T BELIEVE IT. "SEVEN WEEKS! YOU'LL HAVE TO SHIP THE CAST TO ME. I'LL LEAVE A BOX."

"YOU'RE NUTS," I TOLD HIM.

"I BET IT ITCHES LIKE TERMITES."

"IT DOES."

"YOU COULD JAM A COAT HANGER DOWN IN THERE."

HENRY IS A GREAT CARD PLAYER. HE HAS THIS MADDENING WAY OF DISTRACTING EVERYONE WITH ALL SORTS OF MINDLESS SMALL TALK. HE'D NEVER ADMIT IT,

BUT I'M SURE THIS IS PART OF HIS STRATEGY. IT'S HARD TO CONCENTRATE WHEN SOMEONE'S TALKING ABOUT HAVING AN EMPTY CAST SHIPPED TO NEW YORK. I STARTED THINKING ABOUT WHAT THE BOX WOULD LOOK LIKE. I WONDERED WHAT HIS TWELVE GIRLFRIENDS WOULD SAY WHEN THEY SAW THE CAST PROPPED UP AGAINST THE WALL IN HIS APARTMENT. I STARTED FEELING ALMOST POSITIVE THERE WERE BUGS CRAWLING AROUND INSIDE MY CAST. I BEGGED MY DAD TO GO GET ME A COAT HANGER. AND ALL THE WHILE I MADE STUPID PLAYS ALL OVER THE CRIBBAGE BOARD.

EVENTUALLY I GOT MY COAT HANGER STRAIGHTENED OUT AND JAMMED IT ALL THE WAY DOWN TO MY KNEECAP. THAT WAS AN IMPROVEMENT. WE BASICALLY SAT THERE PLAYING CARDS FOR ABOUT AN HOUR, TALKING ABOUT NOTHING IN PARTICULAR — MOSTLY, HENRY WAS TRYING TO THROW US OFF, AND WAS DOING A HIT-OR-MISS JOB. EVENTUALLY MOM CAME HOME, AND AFTER CALLING HELLOS, WE HEARD HER POUNDING AWAY ON THE PIPES IN THE KITCHEN.

"YOU SHOULD GO HELP HER," HENRY SAID.

Henry has a lot of sympathy for my mom. He knows my dad isn't very good about taking on home projects. My dad is plenty capable, but he lacks motivation for certain kinds of tasks.

"You go help her," Dad said.

"What's she doing in there?" Henry asked.

"Trying to unclog the garbage disposal," my dad said. "She's under the sink, hitting the pipe with a rolling pin. Believe it or not, it usually works."

"Sounds a little like the old dredge when it was really cranking."

My mom started yelling at the sink, which prompted my dad to set his cards down, sigh deeply, and walk indifferently to her rescue.

There was something about that noise — the sound of banging on metal — that made me think again of the night I'd fallen and smashed my leg. There had been a clanging sound, barely audible, as if someone was hitting metal on metal.

I decided to ask Henry about his comment.

"What sound do you mean?"

HENRY LEANED BACK IN HIS CHAIR UNTIL IT WAS ONLY ON TWO LEGS.

"THE DREDGE WAS INCREDIBLY LOUD. TONS OF ROCKS WERE SCOOPED FROM THE GROUND AND DUMPED INSIDE. THE CONVEYOR BELTS WERE RIMMED WITH THICK PLANKS OF WOOD THAT KEPT EVERYTHING FROM FALLING OUT. IT WAS LIKE A LONG WATER SLIDE — YOU'VE SEEN THOSE? — BUT INSTEAD OF WATER SHOOTING THROUGH, IT WAS BOULDERS. IT ECHOED LIKE MAD, WHICH SEEMED TO QUADRUPLE THE RUMBLING. SUCH A HORRIBLE SOUND. A CREW OF FOUR WAS REQUIRED TO RUN THE DREDGE, AND THEY WERE SEPARATED BY QUITE A DISTANCE. ONE WAS STATIONED AT THE GEARS IN FRONT WHERE THEY WATCHED EVERYTHING COME IN. THAT PERSON GREASED THE MACHINES AND PULLED THE STOP-CHAIN IF THINGS GOT JAMMED UP. ANOTHER WAS AT THE FAR END, WATCHING THE TAILINGS DUMP OUT. THERE WAS A MAN AT THE CONTROL BOOTH AND ONE MORE WE CALLED A ROAMER — A GUY WHO FIXED THINGS ON THE FLY FROM A RUNNING LIST OF PROBLEMS."

"BUT THE SOUND — THE BANGING — WHAT SOUND WAS THAT?"

"The workers couldn't hear one another. They couldn't yell that loud. So they used signals. They banged metal wrenches or hammers against the iron girders of the dredge to tell each other things. It was like Morse code, simple but effective in those days."

When Dad returned, the conversation veered quickly away from the dredge. I didn't want him to hear us talking about it, and maybe Henry didn't, either. Instead, we all played cards and talked about the Yankees and the Mariners. After a while, Mom brought the casserole with the crispy cheese top and the last of the late summer bees started swarming around the porch.

I'VE SPENT A LOT OF TIME AWAY FROM MY BEDROOM TODAY, WHICH MAKES ME FEEL ANXIOUS. I FEEL LIKE THE FBI HAS SCOURED MY MATTRESS AND SQUEAKY BOX SPRING, TAKEN PICTURES, DUSTED FOR FINGERPRINTS — ALL THE WHILE WITH TWO-WAY RADIOS WIRED TO THE KITCHEN SO MOM COULD TELL THEM IF I WAS ON MY WAY AND THEY COULD JUMP OUT THE SECOND-STORY WINDOW. I KNOW THIS SOUNDS STUPID, BUT IT'S HOW I FEEL ALL THE SAME.

THE ROOM APPEARS UNTOUCHED. BEFORE I LEFT I TOOK SARAH'S ADVICE AND FOUND A BETTER HIDING PLACE FOR THIS JOURNAL. I SLID IT INSIDE MY NINTH-GRADE ANNUAL FROM LAST YEAR AND PUT THE ANNUAL BETWEEN A WHOLE BUNCH OF OTHER BOOKS. I ALSO TAPED IT SHUT. IT DOESN'T LOOK TO ME LIKE THEY FOUND IT. THE SEAL HASN'T BEEN BROKEN.

THEY'LL LEAVE ME ALONE FOR A WHILE — HENRY'S GOT ALL THEIR ATTENTION — SO IT'S A GOOD TIME TO EMAIL SARAH AND TELL HER ABOUT WHAT I FOUND IN MY DAD'S DRESSER.

Friday, September 17, 9:20 p.m.

Too late, she already emailed me. It was a short, bad email. The worst kind.

I'm going back tonight. I have to. Don't worry — I'm fine. I'll contact you tomorrow. Delete this!   S

So I emailed her back.

Sarah,
Have you lost your mind? Don't get anywhere near the dredge right now! People are probably watching. And besides that, I'm digging up all sorts of reasons to stay clear of that thing (as if a phantom isn't reason enough!). I found something in my dad's room. You're amazed I went in there, right? Me too. Trust me, it was insane. I attached a scan of what I found. It feels like dangerous information to have. It will ring a bell from the ads we found in the old newspapers about the Crossbones. I think they're still meeting. I think my dad is one of them. Did I mention that I'm shaking right now? I'm telling you, Sarah, stay away from the dredge. Don't go back there tonight. We're getting too close.

I found out something else about the sounds I heard that night — I have to get off-line but I'll send it later. I'm still figuring it out.

Stay put!!

Ryan

FRIDAY, SEPTEMBER 17, 9:40 P.M.

IS IT NORMAL TO GET IN THE HABIT OF ERASING EVERYTHING? I GET THE DISTINCT FEELING I'LL BE DOING IT FOR THE REST OF MY LIFE. I'LL GROW UP TO BE A CONSPIRACY THEORIST. THE GOVERNMENT WILL BE OUT TO GET ME. I'LL ERASE MY IDENTITY AND MOVE TO A SOUTH AMERICAN FISHING VILLAGE BUT THEY'LL TRACK ME DOWN AND DRAG ME BACK AND MY PARENTS WILL PUT ME IN A GROUP HOME.

I HATE TECHNOLOGY.

IT'S A GOOD THING I'M WRITING EVERYTHING ON GOOD OLD-FASHIONED PAPER. SOMEONE IS GOING TO FIND THIS AFTER I'M GONE. WHEN YOU GET TO THIS PART AND I'VE DISAPPEARED, GO BACK AND WATCH THE VIDEO OF WHEN I FELL. THE ONE WITH <u>THERAVEN</u> FOR A PASSWORD. LISTEN TO THOSE DISTANT SOUNDS OF METAL ON METAL. I DID. I LISTENED TO THE SOUNDS OVER AND OVER AGAIN, AND NOW I'LL NEVER FORGET THEM EVEN IF I TRY.

GO ON. GO BACK AND LISTEN.

129

Friday, September 17, 10:15 p.m.

I'm feeling less gloomy and more edgy in the last half hour. Surfing online always has that effect on me. It tends to fry my nerves. I found an image with all the Morse code letters and I read all about how the taps and the gaps in sound are supposed to work.

I figured out that what I heard on the dredge was like Morse code, but not entirely the same. The longer sound — the one made by the dash — that one doesn't match up. That's been replaced instead by a different <u>TONE.</u> There are two tones on the dredge that represent the dots and the dashes. I imagine the dots being a hammer hitting iron, and the dashes being a wrench hitting the same spot. The two sounds are different in tone instead of length, so it still works.

This is the message that played on the dredge the night I fell:

.- .-. . | -.-- --- ..- | - .... . | .- .-. -.-. .... . -- .. ... - |

The dots are the hammer, and the bars are the wrench. The message asks a question.

ARE YOU THE ALCHEMIST?

EERIE, RIGHT? I'LL ADMIT — I'M FREAKING OUT. BECAUSE WHEN I WAS MEASURING IT ALL OUT, I DIDN'T THINK IT WOULD ADD UP TO ANYTHING. I THOUGHT IT WOULD BE NONSENSE.

BUT NO.

IT'S A QUESTION.

WHATEVER ASKED THE QUESTION WAS EXPECTING AN ANSWER IT DIDN'T GET. SARAH WON'T KNOW THE ANSWER TONIGHT ANY BETTER THAN SHE DID THE NIGHT OF THE ACCIDENT. MAYBE THE GHOST OF OLD JOE BUSH HAS A MESSAGE FOR SOMEONE — THE ALCHEMIST. IT WOULD BE USEFUL IF I KNEW WHAT AN ALCHEMIST WAS.

AND THERE'S THE PIECE OF PAPER I FOUND.

THE ALCHEMIST DIAGRAM OF 79 FOR PAUL McCRAY

PAUL McCRAY. THAT'S MY DAD. SO THERE'S NO DOUBT ANYMORE. MY DAD IS SOMEHOW ENTANGLED IN THIS MESS, AND SO IS THE CROSSBONES. WAS MY DAD MAKING THE SOUNDS? IF SO, MAYBE THE GHOST OF OLD JOE BUSH IS TRYING TO MAKE CONTACT, TRYING TO FIND SOMETHING OR SOMEONE.

ARE YOU THE ALCHEMIST?

What about Daryl Bonner? He looks like Old Joe Bush. He could be the alchemist.

What would happen if I knew the answer and I gave it to Old Joe Bush on the dredge? What would he tell me? What would he do to me?

Whatever it was that made the sounds that night saw Sarah and me as intruders in its secret domain. We didn't understand the question, so we didn't reply. And because of that, it got angry and came for me.

I need to make sure Sarah doesn't go back there again.

She <u>can't</u> go back.

Not ever.

Friday, September 17, 10:41 p.m.

My parents have turned in and Henry is in the guest room downstairs. It's been a long day of fishing, cards, and comfort food. They'll all be tired. I can't just sit here. Sarah could already be at the dredge or about to leave. I have to get out of here. The walk to her house isn't that far, half a mile. I could do it with my crutches. Maybe. I could tap on her window like the raven and she'd be safe because she wouldn't go. She's not the alchemist. She can't go in there if she's not the alchemist or she might never come out. I could wake up tomorrow morning and she'd be gone. No one would know where she went.

I MADE IT TO THE BOTTOM OF THE STAIRS THIS
TIME. IT WAS DARK, SO IT WAS SLOW GOING, BUT
I MADE IT WITHOUT KNOCKING ANYTHING OVER. I
BUMPED THE COFFEE TABLE WITH MY CAST AND
IT MADE A SOUND, BUT NO ONE STIRRED.

I OPENED THE FRONT DOOR TO THE PORCH
AS QUIETLY AS I COULD. THE SCREEN DOOR
REMAINED CLOSED IN FRONT OF ME, AND THIS I
KNEW WAS A MORE COMPLICATED MATTER. IT'S
OLD AND SQUEAKY. ANOTHER OF THOSE HOME
PROJECTS MY DAD NEVER GOT AROUND TO
FIXING. SO I WENT ABOUT OPENING THE SCREEN
DOOR VERY SLOWLY, UNTIL THERE WAS A GAP
BIG ENOUGH FOR ME AND MY LUMBERING CAST
TO FIT THROUGH.

IT GETS REALLY COLD AT THE BASE OF THE
MOUNTAIN AT NIGHT IN THE FALL — WE'RE AT

5,200 FEET. I WAS THINKING ABOUT HOW COLD IT MUST BE — WAS IT 30 OR 35 DEGREES OUTSIDE? SOMETHING LIKE THAT. 70 DURING THE DAY AND BITTER COLD AT NIGHT — THAT'S FALL IN SKELETON CREEK.

When I passed through the gap my cast touched the floorboards and they creaked. That's when I heard the voice.

"Hey, partner! Must be hot upstairs. Your mom's got the heat blasting in there."

It was Henry with a bottle in one hand, lying on the old couch, covered in an even older blanket.

"There's no air like this in New York. Not even one breath full."

"I never thought of it that way."

"Well, it's true. When I retire, I'm going to permanently plant my butt on this couch."

"Better talk to my mom. She might sell it."

"She wouldn't. Would she?"

We small-talked a little bit more and then I said I was going back to bed.

"Let me help you up those stairs."

"It's okay — really — I want to do it alone. If you hear a crash, come running. Otherwise, I'll be fine."

"Suit yourself."

I WENT BACK INSIDE, PAST THE LIVING ROOM AND THE DINING ROOM AND INTO THE KITCHEN AT THE BACK OF THE HOUSE. WE HAVE A YELLOW PHONE IN THERE THAT HANGS ON THE WALL, AND I DIALED SARAH'S NUMBER. I KNOW — STUPID — BUT I WAS OUT OF OPTIONS. IT WAS A TERRIBLE RISK, BUT I TRULY FELT SHE WAS IN TROUBLE. IF KEEPING HER SAFE MEANT GIVING HER UP, THEN I WAS READY TO PAY THAT PRICE.

IT RANG FOUR TIMES AND I ALMOST HUNG UP. SARAH'S MOM ANSWERED. SHE SOUNDED LIKE I WOKE HER.

"HELLO?"

ALREADY IT FELT LIKE A MISTAKE. BUT I HAD TO KEEP GOING.

"HI, MRS. FINCHER. IT'S ME, RYAN."

"ARE YOU OKAY? WHAT'S WRONG?"

"I WOKE UP WORRIED ABOUT SARAH. I DON'T KNOW WHY. COULD YOU DO ME A FAVOR AND MAKE SURE SHE'S OKAY?"

"HANG ON."

THERE WAS A LONG PAUSE IN WHICH I THOUGHT I

WOULD CRAWL OUT OF MY OWN SKIN. MY PARENTS
COULD COME DOWN ANY SECOND. SARAH COULD BE
GONE. HENRY COULD WALK IN. . . .

AFTER ABOUT TEN YEARS, SARAH'S MOM CAME
BACK ON THE LINE.

"SHE'S ASLEEP."

"OH, THAT'S GREAT. OKAY, I'M FINE NOW — SORRY
TO BOTHER YOU. REALLY SORRY."

"RYAN, YOU CAN'T BE CALLING HERE. YOU
KNOW THAT."

"PLEASE DON'T TELL MY PARENTS — I WAS JUST
WORRIED — I HAVEN'T TALKED TO HER IN A WHILE."

"HOW ARE YOU HOLDING UP?"

"GREAT! I'M JUST GREAT, MRS. FINCHER. THE LEG
FEELS MUCH BETTER. THANKS FOR ASKING."

"GOOD NIGHT, RYAN."

"NIGHT."

I DON'T THINK SHE'S GOING TO TELL THEM. OR
MAYBE THAT'S JUST MY HOPE TALKING.

I WENT BACK TO MY ROOM AS QUIETLY AS I COULD,
WHICH TOOK A LONG TIME. WHEN I GOT BACK IN BED, I
FELT A WAVE OF RELIEF.

Now, reading this over, I'm not sure. I think I did the right thing.

All the other troubles in my life don't matter as long as I know Sarah is safe.

The truth about Skeleton Creek is not worth dying for.

Saturday, September 18, 7:21 p.m.

I don't remember falling asleep. I woke to find this journal sitting at the foot of my bed with the pen tucked inside. Did I do that? I don't think I did. Someone came in here and read it.

There's no other explanation.

I know this because I don't put the pen in like that and because I would never set it on the edge of my bed. It was Dad or Mom. Either way, I'm doomed. It's so much harder to be careful when I'm too tired to keep my eyes open.

SATURDAY, SEPTEMBER 18, 7:35 A.M.

I JUST CHECKED MY EMAIL, AND SARAH'S SENT ME ANOTHER VIDEO.

SARAHFINCHER.COM
PASSWORD:
PETERQUINT

Saturday, September 18, 7:38 a.m.

She's driving me crazy! Someone needs to get her under control. I can't believe she actually went to the dredge — and that she's planning on going back.

Doesn't she understand why I called last night?

Doesn't she realize she could get hurt? Or worse?

And I can't believe she's going to make me wait to see what she found out yesterday. That's such a Sarah thing to do — make me feel even more stuck than I felt before. It makes me furious when she holds out on me. She knows that. What I want to do is get my crutches and walk to her house. I'd tell her face-to-face to stop feeding me information with a spoon. What am I, a two-year-old? And while I was at it, I'd tell her to stop being so reckless. It's the same thing all over again, only this time it will be her that gets hurt.

(Is it me, or am I starting to sound a lot like my dad?)

Saturday, September 18, 7:53 a.m.

Sometimes I feel like Sarah is a lit match and I'm a stick of dynamite. Whatever it is that's drawing us together will eventually lead to an explosion.

No, wait — that's not it — it's different. It's more like Sarah and I are polar opposites being pulled toward the same dangerous middle. Why can't we be drawn together by something safe — like raising a cow for the state fair?

Why does everything have to be so dangerous?

Saturday, September 18, 8:15 a.m.

Because a cow is a dull animal and raising one would be a dull undertaking.

Dangerous is more exciting.

Saturday, September 18, 8:35 a.m.

The truth is I'm just mad because I can't stand it that she's having all the adventure and I'm stuck at home with this stupid cast and my meddling parents. She's my best friend and it's hard to be apart and to worry about her. And plus I miss her and I guess I'm lonely.

I'm going online to figure out what an alchemist is.

Saturday, September 18, 8:55 a.m.

I've got a lot of studying to do. Alchemy is . . . deep and wide. Precious metals like gold and silver play an important part. Very interesting.

Today I have to drive all the way into the city with my mom to see the doctor. He's on call on Saturday mornings, so it worked out to have Mom drive me when she didn't have to work. We're leaving in half an hour, so I've only had time to print out a chart I found. I'm sticking it in here. I need to send an email to Sarah, too, so she can see this.

He's going to let me get out more — the doctor, I mean. I'm sure of it. Then I'll feel better. Then I can do more. I could be useful. I could look around town for the alchemist or the secret society. I could even go to the dredge if I wanted to.

I've felt this way before. I know what's going on here.

Sarah's dragging me back in again.

146

SATURDAY, SEPTEMBER 18, 9:15 A.M.

THIS IS WHAT I JUST WROTE TO HER.

Sarah,

I'm out all day visiting the doctor but I'll be back by six and I'll go straight to my room so I can see what you've found. I wish you'd just told me. When I find things, I tell you right away — why can't you do the same? I understand you want to show me, not tell me, when you discover things, but it's frustrating from over here!

I can get around better. I'm getting used to walking. I'm slow, and stairs are a problem, but I can definitely get out of the house. If you go to the dredge again, I want in. I'm not letting you go out there all by yourself anymore. We have to stick together, even if it feels like the whole world is trying to keep us apart.

Someone was sending us a message that night, but we didn't understand it. Do you remember the clanging sounds? Henry told me the workers used to bang on metal to tell each other things because the machinery was so loud. Those sounds that night — they were a question.

Are you the alchemist?

I found the attached file this morning at an alchemy site. I'm not sure what to make of it.

Do you see it? Do you see the birdie?

Let's stay together on this, okay? No more running around at night alone in the woods.

Ryan.

147

AND THEN I SHOWED HER THE SYMBOLS.

Alchemy Symbolism

Antimony
Wild spirit of man
in the form of a wolf

Arsenic
In the everlasting
image of the swan

Bismuth
Undetermined
ancient usage

Copper
One of the seven
metals of Alchemy

Gold
The perfection of everything -
all matter, mind, and spirit

Iron
One of the seven
metals of Alchemy

Lead
One of the seven
metals of Alchemy

Magnesium
One of the seven
metals of Alchemy

Mercury
One of the seven
metals of Alchemy

Platinum
Gold and Silver as one

Potash
Potassium Carbonate

Silver
One of the seven
metals of Alchemy

Sulfur
One of the three
heavenly substances

Tin
One of the seven
metals of Alchemy

Zinc
Philosopher's
wool - the white snow

148

We have a minivan, which my dad hates and will not drive. I personally like minivans. If you ask me, they get a bad rap. I like that both rows of seats come out and, with the doors shut, a whole sofa fits in there. I can see where that would be handy. And when we go on a long drive, there's room to roam. I don't have to sit in one place all the time. I'm restless, so I appreciate the options.

Having a really long cast on my leg has given me a whole new reason to appreciate the spaciousness of this vehicle. Henry and my dad took the middle seats out and I'm sitting all the way in the back. Plenty of room to rest my leg, and I can write in peace back here. The suspension on this van is really pretty good. A writer can tell.

Saturday, September 18, 1:15 p.m.

Okay I'm alone in the examining room, or whatever they call it. Since I didn't want to risk anyone seeing the journal, I'm writing this in a regular notebook. I'll paste these pages (and the page from the van) into the journal later.

This was definitely a good idea. Because when I took the notebook out to write about the minivan — not exactly the most controversial of subjects — Mom kept looking in the rearview mirror. I could tell she wanted to know what I was writing. Maybe she was extra curious because she was the one who sneaked in and looked at my journal before. Maybe she was thinking she'd have to take a look at this new one soon.

It's the pits not being able to trust your own parents.

Finally, while I was writing about the van's suspension, she came right out and asked, "What're you writing there, Ryan?"

"Just stories," I said. "Maybe I'll show them to you one day."

"So you keep telling me."

I pretended to joke with her. "Then you haven't read them?" I said lightly.

Her tone was just as jokey. "Nope. Too busy feeding Henry and sorting mail."

"So I can trust you?"

Then she got all serious.

"It's like faith," she said. "You just have to believe. I can't prove it to you."

This was, I think, a good answer.

"Do you think dad has read my stories?" I ventured.

She met my eye briefly in the rearview mirror, then looked back to the road. "If he has, he's the biggest hypocrite in three counties. You know how he respects privacy. Worth its weight in gold, right?"

"Right."

We drove a little bit more in silence. I wondered what she was thinking, because the next thing she asked was, "Have you emailed Sarah?"

I lied and told her I hadn't.

"Trust goes both ways, you know," she said.

I told her I knew.

Being friends with Sarah makes me a liar.

There's no way around it.

Why does everything have to be so complicated?

Saturday, September 18, 5:20 p.m.

Driving home now.

Mom is watching. But I'm too far back for her to be able to read anything.

Everything went fine at the hospital. The doctor cut the hard cast off my leg and replaced it with one that straps on even tighter than plaster. He made me promise to keep it on unless I'm in the shower (and even there I have to sit down on a chair). I asked the doctor if I could keep the cast and he said I could. I'm very excited to get home and surprise Henry with it.

The doctor wants me to start walking around more, which is both good and bad since I'll probably be going to the dredge tonight. Good because I'll have a little more mobility with the lighter leg brace, bad because I'm more likely to reinjure myself if I have a reason to run away.

It's been a quiet drive home and I've been thinking about everything. So much has piled up in the past couple of days, I haven't taken the time to try and piece it all together. I'm afraid of going back, especially at night. I don't want to

SEE OLD JOE BUSH COME OUT OF THE BLACK POND.
WHAT IF HE GRABS ME THIS TIME? EVER SINCE I TOLD
SARAH I'D GO WITH HER, I'VE BEEN THINKING THAT HE'LL
GET ME AND DRAG ME DOWN INTO THE WATER WITH HIM.
WHAT A NIGHTMARE.

I FEEL CERTAIN EVERYTHING IS CONNECTED, LIKE
SARAH SAID. THE DREDGE, MY DAD, THE CROSSBONES,
THE ALCHEMIST, THE GHOST OF OLD JOE BUSH, EVEN
RANGER BONNER. I'M STARTING TO WORK ON A
THEORY I'LL TELL SARAH TONIGHT.

THE WORST THING I HAVE TO FACE IS THAT THE
DREDGE REALLY IS HAUNTED, AND THAT I PROBABLY
HAVE TO GO BACK THERE. I WONDER IF I'LL DRAG MY
LEG, AND OLD JOE BUSH WILL THINK I'M MAKING FUN
OF HIM. HE WON'T LIKE THAT.

Saturday, September 18, 7:10 p.m.

There are too many people around. I can't risk checking the computer. I barely made it off the porch!

Okay — I'll admit it.

I'm hiding in the bathroom, so I can at least have time to write a few things down.

I am DYING to get to my room and hear from Sarah. I can only hope my mom and dad don't go up there, check my email, and see that Sarah has sent me a video to watch. That would be a catastrophe.

But they're pretty busy right now, so I think I'm okay.

Henry and Dad caught two monster steelhead today and decided to have a fish feed on the front porch. I hate fish feeds. About a million neighbors have come overr with potato salad, coleslaw, baked beans, and potato chips.

I'VE BEEN SITTING ON THE GOLD COUCH FOR OVER AN HOUR SUFFERING QUESTION AFTER QUESTION ABOUT MY ACCIDENT. NOBODY WANTS TO COME RIGHT OUT AND ASK WHAT I WAS DOING AT THE DREDGE, BUT I CAN TELL THEY WANT TO KNOW. I CAN TELL THEY HAVE THEORIES.

NOBODY MENTIONS SARAH'S NAME. ALL THESE NEIGHBORS WHO'VE SEEN US GROW UP TOGETHER.

NOT A SINGLE ONE.

I KNOW I CAN'T STAY IN HERE FOREVER, BUT IT'S THE ONLY PLACE PEOPLE WILL LEAVE ME ALONE. IT'S COOLING DOWN OUTSIDE, BUT A FISH FEED IS A BIG DEAL IN A TOWN AS DULL AS SKELETON CREEK. NO ONE'S LIKELY TO LEAVE UNTIL THEIR TEETH START CHATTERING. THERE'S AN OPPRESSIVE FEELING OF SECRECY IN THE AIR, AND IT'S INTENSIFIED BY THE SIZE OF THE CROWD.

WHEN I WAS FIVE, DAD TOOK ME FISHING ON THE CREEK. HE HOOKED A NICE TROUT AND HANDED ME THE

ROD. WE DRAGGED IT IN TOGETHER, HIS BIG HAND OVER MINE ON THE REEL. THEN HE TOOK THE FISH OFF THE HOOK AND BASHED ITS HEAD AGAINST A ROCK UNTIL IT WAS DEAD. I CRIED ALL THE WAY HOME.

I ALWAYS THROW ALL MY FISH BACK. AFTER I CATCH THEM, I MEAN — I THROW THEM BACK.

I'D RATHER HOLD A FISH UNDERWATER AFTER I CATCH IT AND LET IT PUMP ITS GILLS IN MY HAND UNTIL IT'S READY TO SWIM OFF. I TALK TO THE FISH I CATCH: BE CAREFUL NOW. I'M A NICE FISHERMAN, BUT THE NEXT GUY MIGHT TAKE YOU HOME AND COOK YOU. TELL YOUR BUDDIES.

IT MAKES ME SAD THE WAY WE KILL THINGS WITHOUT ANY REASON. WHY BEAT THE LIFE OUT OF A WILD TROUT WHEN THERE'S PERFECTLY GOOD CANNED TUNA DOWN AT THE STORE?

HENRY IS HAVING A POKER PARTY TONIGHT. HE WAS THRILLED TO HAVE MY OLD CAST AT HIS DISPOSAL AND THANKED ME ENDLESSLY. CARDS WILL PROBABLY GO UNITL ABOUT MIDNIGHT, WHICH MEANS IT WON'T BE SAFE FOR ME

TO LEAVE THE HOUSE FOR A LONG TIME.

I NEED TO TELL SARAH.

GLADYS THE LIBRARIAN SHOWED UP AT THE FISH FEED WITH A BAG OF CARROTS. SHE CAME OVER A HALF HOUR AGO AND HELD ONE OUT TO ME.

"EAT ONE OF THESE. IT'LL HELP YOU SEE TROUBLE COMING," SHE SAID.

ALL I COULD SPUTTER OUT WAS, "YES MA'AM."

I GOT THE CHILLS WHEN SHE TURNED TO GO. I WAS THINKING IN TERMS OF THE ALCHEMIST DIAGRAM OF 79.

THE FLOOR AND 7TH, FOUR PAST THE NINE ON DOOR NUMBER TWO = LIBRARY ATTIC, ENTER THROUGH THE ALLEY DOOR MARKED 213.

I FEEL LIKE SHE'S INVOLVED. BUT HOW?

OUR PARK RANGER, DARYL BONNER, ALSO SHOWED UP. IT WAS STRANGE TO SEE HIM, BECAUSE I HAD TO PRETEND I DIDN'T KNOW WHAT HE LOOKED LIKE. I ACTUALLY WENT OUT OF MY WAY TO ASK MY DAD WHO HE WAS. LUCKILY, HE WASN'T WEARING A PARK RANGER OUTFIT OR ANYTHING, SO I

DIDN'T SOUND TOO OUT OF IT. HE BROUGHT A FROZEN GARDENBURGER WITH HIM, AND MY DAD DROPPED IT ON THE GRILL LIKE A HOCKEY PUCK. THE TWO OF THEM TALKED QUIETLY UNTIL HENRY CAME OVER AND GAVE BONNER A HARD TIME.

"THOSE ARE MADE OF DOG FOOD," HENRY SAID. "DID YOU KNOW THAT?"

"I HADN'T HEARD."

ALL THREE OF THEM SWIGGED THEIR DRINKS AND STARED AT THE HOCKEY PUCK ON THE GRILL.

"WE JUST HAD OUR FOURTH PLAYER DROP OUT. CARE TO PLAY CARDS TONIGHT?"

"I'D BE DELIGHTED."

"BRING ONE OF THOSE FROZEN FRISBEES. I HAVE AN IDEA I COULD USE ONE."

BEING NEW IN TOWN, DARYL HAS NO IDEA THAT HENRY MIGHT BE DUCT-TAPING THE FROZEN GARDENBURGER TO HIS FOREHEAD BEFORE THE NIGHT IS OVER. I FEEL A LITTLE SORRY FOR HIM.

And I also feel really strange that we're under the same roof.

I think I'm going to tell my mom I'm tired. Maybe she'll let me go upstairs and lie down.

There's enough noise that it'll make sense for my door to be closed.

I just hope they won't realize it's also locked.

Saturday, September 18, 7:30 p.m.

My clothes smell like fried fish, which makes me mad at Henry and Dad for going on a killing spree on the river today. You'd think grown men would know better.

It doesn't seem like anyone's been in here. I mean, Dad's been with Henry and I've been with Mom. I should be safe. Plus, they assume there's no activity because I haven't been here. But Sarah's sent me a new password. Finally I'll get to see what she hinted at this morning.

Ryan,

Nice detective work on the alchemist chart. Did you know 79 is the chemical element number for gold? I looked it up. I guess it should stand to reason that everything secret in this town would revolve around gold. Do you think there's a hidden stash of it somewhere?

Sorry I've been mysterious about showing you this, but you're right - it has to be shown, not told.

More talk in the video, especially about visiting the dredge. Password: lucywestenra

Sarah.

I've heard that name — Lucy Westenra — but I can't place it. Who is that? Peter Quint, I knew — but Lucy . . . I know I've heard that name before. I'll have to look it up later.

Now, I have to go watch a video.

SARAHFINCHER.COM
PASSWORD:
LUCYWESTENRA

Saturday, September 18, 7:55 p.m.

This is too much.

Sarah thinks Joe Bush was killed by the Alchemist.

But we don't know who the alchemist is, or even if there's only one of them.

And she thinks Joe Bush's ghost is guarding something. Well, not exactly guarding. He's haunting the place where the alchemist keeps his secrets. Waiting to take revenge.

But what about the dredge? Waht about that secret handle she seems to have found, which appears to have vanished between then and now, in a place that was supposedly untouched?

What about what I saw?

She can't go back there.

It's too dangerous.

Especially if she's alone.

I can't believe I'm even thinking about going back.

IN MY CONDITION.

BUT THERE WON'T BE ANY WAY TO STOP HER, SHORT OF CALLING IN OUR PARENTS. AND I CAN'T DO THAT. THAT WOULD BE THE END OF EVERYTHING. I HAVE TO GET THERE MYSELF.

IT'S ALREADY DARK. PRETTY SOON SOMEONE WILL BE WEARING MY CAST AT THE POKER TABLE, HOLDING THEIR CARDS WITH OVEN MITTS. I CAN GO DOWN THERE AND WATCH FOR AN HOUR AND SEE IF I CAN GUESS HOW LATE THEY'LL GO. SOME OF THE PLAYERS ARE PRETTY OLD, SO HOPEFULLY THINGS WILL BREAK UP BY MIDNIGHT. WHICH WILL GIVE ME OVER AN HOUR.

OKAY, I JUST EMAILED SARAH. THIS IS WHAT I SAID.

Sarah,

I'm going with you and that's final. Pick me up in the alley behind the house at 1:45AM. I'll be the the one with the brace on his leg.

Can't wait to see you.

Ryan

Saturday, September 18, 10:00 p.m.

I just went downstairs without telling anyone so I could see how fast I'd get to the bottom without making any noise or falling on my face. No one saw me, so I did it twice. The second time was slower and more painful than the first, but that was mostly because I'd just come back up and I was winded. The brace is still big and heavy but I can move a little better. I think I can do this. If I take one of the crutches with me I'll be fine.

When I arrived on the porch, the poker game was in full swing. The burn barrel had been moved up next to the card table where it blazed with warmth and orange light. Ranger Bonner was wearing a football helmet, and when he nodded in my direction it wobbled up and down over his brow. I felt like everyone was taking turns staring at me, like they were trying to have a good time but my being there made them suspicious. Ranger Bonner and my dad especially.

They kept glancing at each other, then at me. It was very unnerving.

I felt like I was ruining Henry's card game, so I lied and said I was turning in for the night. No one tried to stop me.

I give it another hour — two at the most — and my mom will tell everyone to clear out.

No word yet from Sarah. Where is she?

Saturday, September 18, 11:00 p.m.

The card game broke up early and I'm getting a bad case of the shakes. It's dark outside. My window is a sheet of black in which I keep imagining Old Joe Bush's face peering in, watching me, water dripping off his nose. Or is it blood? I can't tell. It's too dark out there.

That's one thing about a very small town: it's extremely dark at night. Ther are only three streetlights and none of them are near my front door. The moon is also absent tonight, so I'm sure the woods will be especially dark.

That is, if I make it to the woods. Getting out of the house is going to be a trick. Our house was built about a million years ago and it makes old house sounds, the kind that wake parents up. There are seven squeaky steps on the staircase alone.

My hands are so clammy I keep having to stop writing and wipe them on my sheet.

I'M NOT SURE I CAN DO THIS.

FINALLY, AN EMAIL.

Ryan,

Come and see. Password: miltonarbogast

Sarah.

Saturday, September 18, 12:22 p.m.

It appears that I'll be sneaking out of the house tonight to see the one person my parents have forbidden me to associate with. The two of us will wander off into the woods at 1:00 in the morning and cut through a chain so we can break into a condemned structure before they burn it down. And, meanwhile, her camera will be feeding the footage back to her web site so that if we don't come back, the authorities can — what was her phrase? — oh, yeah — find our bodies.

Has Sarah lost it?

What am I doing?

If I get caught, my parents won't just move me to a new town, they'll ground me for a hundred years and feed me boiled beans for breakfast, lunch, and dinner for the rest of my life.

Even still, I almost wish I'd get caught. The alternative is definitely worse.

The dredge at night. I'm not even there yet

AND I CAN ALREADY FEEL THE HAUNTED PRESENCE OF A GHOST DRAGGING ITS LEG IN MY DIRECTION, ASKING ME QUESTIONS I CAN'T ANSWER. AND THIS TIME, WHEN THE GHOST OF OLD JOE BUSH COMES FOR ME, I WON'T BE ABLE TO RUN AWAY.

SUNDAY, SEPTEMBER 18, 12:30 A.M.

Ryan,

We're on - meet me where I said at one, then we'll go straight to the dredge.
Check the webcam from your computer (I'll send you the password in a seperate
email). and email me back. You should see me waving.

Delete!! - Sarah

Sunday, September 19, 12:33 a.m.

I checked the site and saw her waving and now I have to go. I'm confused by this turn of events.

My hands are shaking and I can hardly hold my pen. I know why I'm shaking so badly. It's the same reason why I have to go to the dredge tonight. I think Old Joe Bush has snuck into my brain, because there's a nightmare I keep having. Every night I have the nightmare, only I don't tell anyone — I don't even write it down — because it's a really bad one. It's the kind that if someone reads it, they think you're crazy.

Sarah is in the nightmare. We're together on the dredge, going up the decayed stairs. When we reach the top she turns to me and leans in like she's going to kiss me. I'm so surprised by this I lean back and lose my balance and I grab for her arm. The rotted railing breaks free behind me and I can't let her go, even though I try. It's like electricity is holding us together. We're two magnets falling. We roll through the air and she lands beneath me. There is the sound of

smashing bones and then I wake up.

Sunday, September 19, 12:39 a.m.

I just had to stop and think for a second.

I remember struggling over the beginning of this story, rewriting it a dozen times.

There was a moment not long ago when I thought: This is it. I'm dead.

I remember how that opening set just the right tone. The reader would know that something bad had happened, but they wouldn't know what it was. Things came easy after that, but were confusing, too. The Sarah nightmare bothered me.

Now I feel as if I'm driving around at night in the middle of nowhere. I've lost my sense of direction. Did I have all the videos before? Have I been retracing my steps and she's already gone? Maybe tonight is the last chapter of a story I've already lived through.

I'm going to assume for the moment that the nightmare of Sarah crushed beneath me is just that — a nightmare — and that all of what I've been writing is

REAL. I'M GOING TO MAKE THIS GUESS BECAUSE IF WHAT I'VE BEEN WRITING IS NOT THE TRUTH, THEN MY MIND IS TRYING TO HIDE SOMETHING FROM ME. IF I'VE BEEN MAKING ALL THIS UP AND SOMETHING HAPPENED TO SARAH AND IT'S MY FAULT, THEN I WON'T BE ABLE TO LIVE WITH MYSELF.

I'M GOING TO STAND UP AND PUT ALL MY WEIGHT ON MY ONE GOOD LEG AND START DOWN THE DARKENED HALL TOWARD THE STAIRS. WHEN I LOOK OVER MY SHOULDER, OLD JOE BUSH WILL BE OUTSIDE, STARING THROUGH MY BEDROOM WINDOW WITH THE RAVEN ON HIS SHOULDER. HE'LL BE WATCHING ME LEAVE SO THAT HE CAN GO TO THE DREDGE AHEAD OF ME AND WAIT FOR MY ARRIVAL. HE'S FASTER ON ONE GOOD LEG THAN I AM.

WHEN I REACH THE OPENING TO THE STAIRCASE, MY HEART WILL BE POUNDING AND I'LL LOOK DOWN AND SEE THAT THERE IS NO LIGHT. IT WILL BE A LONG FALL IF I MISS A STEP. MY HAND WILL BE SWEATY AND IT WILL SLIDE WHEN I HOLD THE BANISTER. I FEEL LIKE I KNOW THIS ALREADY, LIKE I'VE DONE IT ALL BEFORE.

WORDS AND SOUNDS WILL TUMBLE IN MY TROUBLED

MIND.

The Crossbones. Are you the Alchemist? Daryl Bonner. Gladys with her shotgun. Old Joe Bush. Is that my Dad's name on the paper? A kiss. The sound of smashing bones.

And hanging over it all will be the one word – gold. It's all about the gold, I know it is. Someone killed Joe Bush for the gold and now Joe wants revenge. He won't rest until he gets what he wants.

It will be a slow journey through a quiet house and I have no choice but to leave. I have twenty minutes and it will take every bit to sneak out of hear. I want to take this journal with me but I can't. It will mean I've left the story behind for sure and returned to the real world. I'm leaving it folded into my sheets so they'll find it in the morning if I'm not here.

Please – if you find this – go to sarahfincher.com. Use the password tanginabarrons.

There you'll see what happens next to me and Sarah.

I've got to go now.

SARAHFINCHER.COM
PASSWORD:
TANGINABARRONS

62144803R00104

Made in the USA
Columbia, SC
29 June 2019